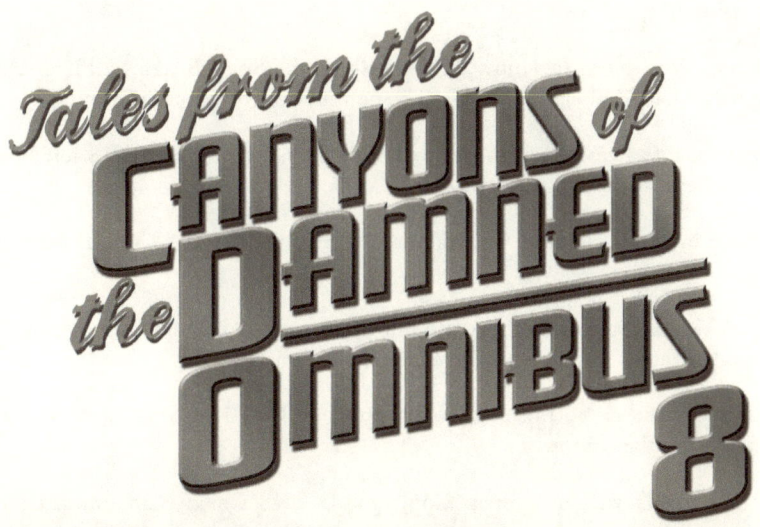

Tales from the **CANYONS** *of the* **DAMNED OMNIBUS 8**

PRESENTED BY USA TODAY BESTSELLING AUTHOR

DANIEL ARTHUR SMITH

Special thanks to Jessica West
Cover Design By Daniel Arthur Smith

  ISBN-13: 978-1-946777-74-4

For Susan, Tristan, & Oliver, as all things are.

26

Tales from the CANYONS of the DAMNED

FEATURING

PHILIP HARRIS

JEFF BOWLES

ERNIE HOWARD

HUNTER C. EDEN

PARANORMAL

PRESENTED BY USA TODAY BESTSELLING AUTHOR

DANIEL ARTHUR SMITH

Catch and Release
Hunter C. Eden

WE'RE DEALING WITH A FAMILY in the suburban Midwest. Dad's about forty, climbing the corporate ladder and just starting to look longingly at the cute intern with the nice legs. Mom's a few years younger, but already wondering what it would have been like if she'd gone for that other guy in college, the one who played guitar and was planning on backpacking across Africa after he graduated. Brother's maybe eight, likes soccer, and is grounded for fighting at school, which at his age means rolling around in the dirt with some other little bastard he called a fag. Sister's six, plans on being a princess when she grows up, and practices hard for it now, the little overachiever. Now which one would you go for?

You probably said Dad or one of the kids. You figure that under your malevolent influence, Dad's going to grab a wood axe and start splitting heads, or maybe sister is going to start vomiting blood and talking about all the things your mother likes doing in Hell. I go for Mom. No one expects it because nobody pays much attention to her anyway. By the time they realize what's going on, I'm in too deep for them to stop me, and I can do what I came here to do.

First thing, when I swim into her soul on Hell's high tide, she starts to get really quiet. Sister's oblivious, Brother's a resentful little shit, and Dad's too busy thinking about that intern, so nobody notices. Dad tells himself she's just depressed, maybe needs a spa day or something. As my malevolent influence spreads, she starts eating raw meat. Next time they go to the pool, she dives in and stays under for two, three minutes, and when the lifeguard goes in after her, she bites him so hard, they have to close the pool for a day or two because of all the blood in the water. As he's getting stitches, he swears Mom had weird slits on her neck (and she did—they're my gills) but they're gone by the time she gets out of the pool.

Then the dreams start. She's standing on the coast of Hell, looking out at the dark breakers filled with the bobbing damned. Then my great, jagged fins break the surface like the sails of a cursed galley. Night after night, she sees it. She starts on the shore, then she's ankle deep, then knee-deep, then the tide comes in up to her waist and pretty soon, she's treading black water with the souls of the condemned, looking down at my vast, serpentine bulk twisting underneath her. Pride's not really my sin, but let's be candid: I'm glorious in my infernal horror. These soulless eyes like flat plates of crude oil; these teeth, long as daggers in a mouth grinning with sick whimsy; a set of hooked tentacles for a tongue…I'm everything you imagine swimming just below your feet when you can't see the bottom. I wish I could help Mom take a step back and see how rare it is to be possessed by something like me. She deserves to appreciate the exquisite horror that she's doing so much to bring into the world. I should just use her and discard her, but underneath it all, I'm a big softie.

We'll skip the consultations with doctors and shrinks that turn up nothing. We'll skip the moment where bratty little Brother sees Mom eating Sister's guinea pig with my mouth, chunks of its billowing flesh floating in her transparent stomach. That's when these dumb assholes realize it's not her thyroid or menopause.

What they need is an exorcist.

You may wonder why we do this. It's a lot of shit to go through just to spend a couple weeks inside a soccer mom, right? That's where the Mate comes in.

I meet *her* at a shitty motel with half the letters out in the sign: -OT-L. The parking lot looks like the high-tide line of human misery, awash with old McDonalds bags, used condoms, and needles. As long as we're being honest, I'm way out of *her* league. Wouldn't give *her* a second glance if we'd crossed paths in Hell, in our true forms. *She's* wearing a new number that doesn't exactly flatter her seal-like form: mid-twenties with his blond hair cut in a fauxhawk. A bit of a beer gut.

You could believe he'd be curious about the harried but decently attractive WASPette I'm wearing. It's a bit more of a stretch to think that she'd go for him, but a decade of married sex as exciting as bilgewater and maybe she'd be desperate enough to give him a shot. Especially given how excitedly Dad talks about that smart new intern and her round, full qualifications.

"Hey baby—looking MILFy," *she* says through his mouth.

"Don't start that corny shit," I say to *her*.

"You don't want me to be your toned little pool boy?"

Some of us get really into this, like pretending to be some no-account mortal stoner and a bored housewife is exciting. If I wanted fun, I would've stayed in Hell. It never feels good anyway, wearing a human being. Less intimate.

She dangles the key from his pointer finger, the diamond-shaped fob swaying like a hanged man. Room 666. Dagon almighty, is *she* corny.

"Toned little pool boys do more sit-ups and eat fewer Doritos. Come on."

She sidles up next to me, smacks Mom's ass, and whispers, "I'm really loving this dismissive bitch act. You've got him harder than a priest in a boy scout troop."

"Look, we've probably only got an hour, maybe two max, before her husband finds her here. I get that this is your thing, but I'm here to perpetuate our unholy kind and swim home as soon as the tide goes out, so if we could hurry…"

His lips grin wide, the corners of his mouth touching his ears, showing off *her* needle-like fangs.

"Did I say boy scout troop? More like boy scout jamboree."

The room's what you'd expect. There's a big snarl of hair floating in the toilet and something stained the wall right above the TV a yellowish brown. As for the bed, well, I'm glad it's not my body lying there.

"Let's order some porn, baby," *she* says in her best dudebro voice.

"Let's get this shit over with."

By the time we've stripped down, I'm a little more into it. The big fishy eye *she* grew in his navel, unblinking and cold, the lamprey fangs on the end of his cock—you know how you meet someone sometimes, and they seem like a dud, but then you're surprised by how attracted you are to them? I'm not saying I wouldn't rather do this in Hell with

3

someone else, but we're expected to breed once a century, so I might as well just relax and enjoy myself.

For all *her* corny bullshit, *she's* pretty good—even when we're wearing humans. *She* bites me, leaves big semicircles of needle toothmarks all over Mom's rough, skate-like skin. Bloody water drips from the walls, covering us as we coil around each other in the sheets, bedbugs skittering to escape the ferocity of our impure passion. I lengthen Mom's torso, lashing back and forth in ecstasy like an eel. I'm not making you uncomfortable, am I?

She lights a cigarette with his hands when we're done. If *she* wasn't as good as *she* was, I'd probably get up and leave, but I'll indulge this. I can't believe I'm doing it, but I turn to *her* and say, "So how would you feel about maybe meeting up in Hell sometime? I'm just off the coast of the Archipelago of Lamentation, and—"

And that's when Dad and the exorcist find us. It's too late, of course. Now it's time for the usual routine. A little holy water, a little potty-mouth, I swim home when the tides are right, and they think all that power-of-[insert deity here]-compels-you shit worked.

Except as soon as he comes in, I realize things are different. This ain't your regular priest, imam, swami, or rabbi. He's got a beat-up Bass Pro Shop hat on his head, and a shirt covers his big belly that says Women Want Me, Fish Fear Me. Half that statement is true: I'm fucking terrified.

"Here she is, Mr...?"

"Just call me Shep."

I know about Shep, and Shep knows what he's doing.

He has a thick chain in his hands. The hook is big and barbed, the size of a meat hook, and baited with a flopping something you might mistake for a small shark or a fetus, depending on how you looked at it. Those letters on the shank? They're verses in the secret alphabet of Hell and what they basically mean is that I have to bite.

"Can you do anything to help her, Mr. Shep?"

"Just Shep." He scratches his gray-streaked beard. "I think I probably can. Let's see what we're dealing with here."

The Mate draws back.

"Hey, man, I don't know what's going on here, but I just came here for—" *she* starts.

"Oh, yes you do." Shep sounds jovial. Just the way you'd expect from a man who took a day off to go fishing.

4

She strikes at him, emerging quickly from the stoner's mouth in a flurry of serrated teeth, but he pulls a pendant in the shape of a harpoon out of his shirt. Fuck.

"In Jonah's name!" says Shep, and as *she* recoils in agony, he smiles. "Looks like they're really jumping today. Now, you always want a good, solid chain leader. These bastards'll flat-out bite through a rope."

"Can you please just get it out of her?" says Dad.

"You gotta be patient, son." Shep gives a paternal smile. "Only way anyone gets good at this game. Now, we got a mating pair here, and they tend to get territorial, so we could probably hook them both if you want."

"Mating pair? Did he—did he get her…"

"Naw, they're like salmon, 'cept instead of swimming upstream to the waters they hatched in, they swim into our souls." He pauses, a reflective look on his face. "Which sort of *are* the waters they hatched in, if you think about it."

"I don't care about the other one. Just get Judith back." Dad shakes so violently, you'd think he was possessed himself.

"Well, son, we'll just see what we can do." Shep chuckles as he tosses the hook next to Mom's feet, and I can't help myself. The letters draw me out, and next thing I know, that fucking thing is buried in my jaw. I fight. I thrash around inside her, trying to dig the hook out. I could do it if Shep stopped pulling, but he won't, and the landwalking bastard's having a really good time too. "Hoooo-eeeee! We got a lunker on our hands!"

The Mate bolts out of the hotel room half out of the stoner, but Shep has the one of us he wants, and sooner than I'd like to admit, I'm out of Mom's mouth and lashing on the floor. I'm not giving up without causing some damage, so I lunge at Dad, who screams and stumbles back, filling the air with the ammonia scent of piss.

I coil back, ready to tear his entrails out.

The one thing that saves Dad from having his intestines unraveled all over the crusty carpet is Shep sticking that harpoon pendant in my face. The fucking thing *hurts*, a deep, leaden pain I feel in my eyes, my skin, deep down in my muscles. I writhe around, shattering one of the nightstand lamps with my bulk.

"I put this away, are you going to be good?" Shep dangles the pendant, sways it back and forth like he wants to hypnotize me. I don't have much of a choice, so I just say yes and tell him he can suck Dagon's claspers and swallow when he's done.

"Damn, boy, we got a fighter here! A real beauty." To add insult to injury, the motherfucker kisses me on the snout before he puts the pendant away. But he's right—I'm a symphony of despair and terror given flesh, and that's not such an asset here. See, all true exorcists have a trophy room, and I could be looking at hanging on Shep's wall for eternity.

We can kill each other, but you can't kill us. It's like being in a special club where you get to eat the other members. That was bred into us by Almighty Dagon as a failsafe so some shit-grade televangelist can't pull out a twelve gauge when the Bible verses fail. You do it to us, it heals in minutes, and we're fucking pissed off that you tried.

But there's a problem. Shep's necklace? They call that the Harpoon of Jonah, and it's the one thing you wormfood assholes have against us. You make one big enough, bless it just right, and you can pin one of us to your wall. There's no escaping unless one of you releases us, and the alternative is a harpoon stuck through you for all time. It's like Hell for demons.

I have to convince Shep to let me go, and my position is weak. You never beg, but what am I going to threaten him with? Way I see it, I've got two options.

Option one: buy his soul. Buying souls is a pain in the puckered and barnacle-encrusted orifice that answers for my ass. It's like a deposit that charges no interest, and then you have to go to the trouble of giving the seller whatever he or she wants: money, fame, the hottie they never got in high school, whatever. A lot goes on behind the scenes, believe me. A lot of string-pulling in the mortal world, dark whispers and obscene promises and sheer terror. Besides, what would Shep sell his soul for? What he wants is me on his wall. It'll have to be option two.

There aren't many exorcists in the world, and the number of *real* exorcists, the ones who figure out that a few spritzes of holy water won't do it, are a fraction of a fraction, and the ones who last without getting killed or going insane become legends to us—the sort of thing you warn your spawn about if you don't eat them first. Shep is a legend, which means I know a little bit about him.

Shep grew up in Mississippi, fishing with his Pop. He joined the army, deployed for Iraq One, and that's where he learned about all this.

Found an old manuscript in a bombed-out museum and paid an interpreter to translate it because the pictures of hooks and harpoons, the map of a great and terrible ocean, the diagrams of fish bigger and fiercer and more dangerous than any he'd ever seen, it all interested him. Once he figured out what he was doing, he became one of the best—not because he wanted to purify the world or redeem himself or any of the normal reasons. He just loved performing exorcisms. The thrill of landing one of us got in his blood. He got attached to all this.

So in option two, I play on his biggest weakness: sentimentality.

"Well, Shep, it looks like you reeled me in."

Behind me, Mom is lying on the bed, gasping. I ignore her and Dad. This is all about me and Shep.

"Sure did. Haven't seen one like you in fifteen-odd years. Can't wait to get that grinning head of yours on my wall."

"Demons like me are getting rarer."

"You sure are. Tough to land."

Dad crosses over to where Mom lies on the bed. I snap at him, just to see him jump, and he leads Mom by the hand back to where Shep stands. She's swaying on her feet, only half here.

"Is this over? Do I pay you now?" Dad is still pale with horror.

"Oh, just whatever you can afford, son." Shep smiles and pats Dad on the shoulder. Dad digs into his pockets, pulls out a wallet with trembling hands and pulls out a handful of bills.

"Here."

"Well, thank you," says Shep, grinning. "Now go clean your britches."

Now it's just me and Shep, which is how I want it. He had to put on his exorcist face around Mom and Dad. Pull the Ahab and Moby act. But now I have him where I want him.

"You know, Shep, you're getting older."

"We all do. Well, all us mortals."

"You ever think about the next generation, Shep?"

"What, of you sumbitches? You're with us to the end of time."

"No, I mean you. You got kids, Shep?"

"You know I'm never going to answer that."

I grin at him.

"Yes, you do. And not just kids—*grand*kids. You ever think about getting them into this?"

"I wouldn't get anybody into this." He's pulling a net out of a bag at his feet. I have to do this fast.

"You know how long it took me to grow this big, Shep? You know what it took to get these fangs, these jagged fins, these soulless eyes?"

"That's why I want you on my wall."

"What about the exorcists to come?"

"What about them?" He's unspooling the net, and if he gets it over me—

"Don't you want to leave Hell stocked for them too? Don't you remember the thrill of the first of us you caught? The rush of adrenaline? Don't you want their eyes to light up like yours did the first time? Don't you want their hearts to do that happy, pattering dance of I-can't-believe-I-beached-that-thing?"

He pauses, and the net hangs in his hands. I set the proverbial hook.

"Shep, I'm pregnant." That's how it works. We both become fertile when we don mortal flesh, and we both leave with a belly full of squirming, embryonic horrors implanting in the sickening organ that passes for a womb. "I've probably got about ten eggs in me. One or two will hatch, and they'll eat the rest. Then it takes a good ten millennia to reach my size, and that's no guarantee. After we were cast out of the Pure Waters, the old fertility's not what it used to be. One of these little hellspawns growing inside me is going to get a younger Shep into the game. There's only one thing a good sportsman does here."

"What do you want?"

"For you to do the responsible thing. You're not in this for religion. What do you care? So you can hang me on your wall? That's not you. Catch and release, Shep."

He sighs, looks up from the net. He's torn. He would love to sit under me with a glass of whiskey, reminiscing about our battle. He maybe knows one or two exorcists, and he'd love to brag about me and show me off. But he's too sentimental. In a weird way, I respect him for that. It's all just for the sheer love.

"All right, but next time—"

I give that wide grin, rows upon rows of teeth, and he releases me from the Harpoon's influence. Then I'm swimming free through the black waters of damnation.

Shep will die any year now. He'll probably go to the Pure Waters, which is a disappointment because I would love to turn the tables. I guess he'll always be the one that got away. Such is eternity. Nothing to do but move on to the next soccer mom.

15 Things You Need to Know About Visiting the Spirit Realm

Philip Harris

WITH SALES OF THE iPhone XX reaching stratospheric heights, millions of people around the world now have access to the spirit realm using the brand new integrated RealmScope(tm) chipset. Now, convening with the dead isn't just for psychics and ghostwalkers. Anyone with an up-to-date iSpirit subscription can get down with Grandma Gerta or practice ukulele with Uncle Eustace. With the entire spirit realm open for exploration, you could be forgiven for feeling a little overwhelmed. Which is why we've teamed up with famed spirit realm blogger, Tanya Hurst-Jenkins, to get you up to speed with all things iSpirit. Here's the top 15 things you need to know about RealmScope(tm) and iSpirit.

1) Nathan G. Anderson, a California Institute of Technology graduate researching far spectrum light filters, created the RealmScope(tm) chipset in 2020. A miscalculation during the creation of a quantum lens resulted in a unique, and now patented, distortion in the sub-surface structure of a nano-wave detector. The resultant detector went on to form the heart and soul of the RealmScope(tm) technology.

The mistake proved fortunate, and profitable, for Anderson. The 1,328 patents associated with his research are estimated to have generated over $300 billion worth of revenue for Anderson alone. His sudden elevation to multi-billionaire status reportedly affected his mental well-being, and he has been out of the public eye for several years. Rumors persist that he lives a hermit-like existence on a private island in the Indian ocean.

2) Apple's addition of the RealmScope(tm) to the iPhone is rumored to have cost them $1.3 trillion. Profits from the iPhone XX alone are expected to exceed that within the next two months. Demand was driven, of course, by the now legendary appearance of Apple co-founder, Steve Jobs at the launch of the new device. His impassioned speech broadcast directly from the spirit realm to over seventy countries was not without its controversy, but the voices of the evangelical Christians criticizing the stunt and the RealmScope(tm) itself, were quickly drowned out by the exuberance of the Apple faithful. I was fortunate enough to attend the after-party for the launch, and the atmosphere was electric.

3) The heart of Apple's iSpirit system is the on-device DNA filter that can process a clean DNA sample and initialize the RealmScope(tm) in a fraction of a second. Although there are already dozens of third-party DNA samplers, you'll want to stick with Apple's bluetooth enabled iDNA device available for $1,299. I've tried several different options and take it from me, none of the cheaper systems come close to the build quality and clarity of the results from the Apple device.

4) Whatever sampler you use, gather a range of familial DNA to calibrate the RealmScope(tm). I've found five good samples from living relatives to be the sweet spot. Less than that and transitions to the spirit realm become a little unreliable. Sampling a larger group dilutes the link and you run the risk of finding yourself bumping into inhabitants of the spirit realm that are outside your family tree. Save that for later visits and stick to familiar faces for your first adventures beyond the veil.

5) When you've finished scanning that initial batch of DNA, iSpirit will ask you to register your samples with a central database. This will prevent unauthorized use of your DNA to access the spirit realm. Ancestor theft and the rise of so called realm runners—people who take unauthorized DNA samples and use them to enter the spirit realm—make this an essential step.

It's true that privacy groups have expressed concern over the storage of so much personal DNA in one location and the potential for misuse by government agencies, but Apple has assured users that their DNA information is stored securely and access is only possible through your iPhone XX. Like most people, I was happy to sign up for an iSpirit subscription to ensure that my ancestors only receive visits from those I authorize.

6) A great deal has been made of spirit sickness and a quick Internet search will bring up dozens of supposed cures—everything from crushed dung beetle legs to expensive over-the-counter supplements of questionable veracity.

While it's true you may feel some disorientation during your first visit to the spirit realm, you will quickly acclimatise to it. There's no need to spend hundreds of dollars buying pills and potions (or hours digging around in dung heaps for beetles). Keep your initial trips to just a few minutes then gradually increase your time in the spirit realm until the sickness no longer occurs. A small percentage of people are unable to adjust, but if you're one of those unfortunate few then a simple travel sickness tablet may help. Just be sure to go with a non-drowsy brand so that you don't miss anything juicy while you're on the other side.

7) As you become more comfortable with the spirit realm and the novelty of being able to chat with Aunt Doris about her time as a sniper in World War II begins to fade, it's inevitable that you'll begin looking for other spirits to visit.

The use of DNA to visit the non-ancestral dead is currently a legal gray area. I strongly advise you not to gather DNA at random—there are already a number of pending lawsuits aimed at iSpirit users accused of misappropriating DNA. The most famous of these is that of Miguel Hernández, the Mexican immigrant accused of obtaining the DNA samples of a prominent politician and using it to "right the wrongs of the previous administration," as he put it. Public sympathy in Miguel's plight has grown, but there are other, lower profile cases. Don't be the next one.

8) Licensed DNA brokers are the answer. These accredited businesses undergo a comprehensive range of background checks and you can be

sure that any DNA you buy has been obtained with permission, and that a portion of the fee charged will go directly to the family of the deceased. Contact the National Association of DNA Brokers for details of your local authorized DNA dealer.

And watch out for DNA phishing emails designed to entice you to provide a sample of your own DNA in return for access to funds trapped in an offshore account. These scammers are really just gathering DNA to sell on the black market. Fall for one of these schemes and you may find access to your family tree being sold to the highest bidder.

9) Celebrities are big business in the spirit realm, with the larger chains of DNA brokers snapping up the rights to such luminaries as Humphrey Bogart, Edgar Allan Poe, James Dean, and Audrey Hepburn. Visiting with those big names comes at a hefty price tag.

Marilyn Monroe tops out the list of most expensive stars to hang out with at an eye-watering $447,000 per person for a five minute group visit. Looking for some one-on-one time with the blonde bombshell? You're looking at an eight figure price tag.

Prices do drop considerably with lesser known and television stars coming in at the $10-15,000 mark. Still out of the range of your budget? A private meet and greet with Richard Sloane, who appeared as a background student in the 1988 hit, *Heathers*, can be yours for $199.

Oh, and if anyone comes to you with a great deal on a trip to see Elvis Presley? Walk away. The King's DNA has not yet been recovered after family members discovered the body in the Graceland Meditation Garden was in fact that of Johnny Lanchester, a little-known Elvis impersonator from the late 80s.

10) Do your tastes run a little darker than the King? Criminal DNA may be the answer. Despite considerable uproar from victims, the popularity of serial killers such as Ted Bundy, Aileen Wuornos, Jeffrey Dahmer, and even Tsutomu Miyazaki continues to grow. Prices are increasing but have yet to reach the levels of the big name stars.

Less extreme options are also available and shopping around will often get you a bargain. The International DNA Reserve Corporation are currently offering a 2-for-1 deal on Bonnie Parker and Clyde Barrow, and other companies often run similar promotions.

As part of my "Unlocking the Spirit World" series published in *Time* magazine last year, I spent some quality time with a *very* well known serial killer. Non-disclosure Agreements prevent me from going into too much detail, but the experience was both disturbing and exhilarating. If the idea of immersing yourself in the seedy underbelly of humanity's past appeals, then I highly recommend Darius Dark's DNA Emporium. Their customer service is exemplary, and they were even able to address a few minor concerns I had after my visit.

11) If you enjoy traveling, then a spirit vacation could be just the ticket. Tourists are flocking to destinations all around the world to sample the local cuisine and experience the spirit worlds of other cultures. The most popular destinations include Egypt, Japan, and Peru, but check out your local area, too. Who knows what spirits could be lurking right on your doorstep? Just be sure to stick with a reputable company and ensure they are NADNAB accredited.

12) Although RealmScope(tm) is recommended for adults 21 years or older (19 in some states, check your local legislation), the iSpirit Jr. has proven to be a real hit with 9 to 15-year-olds. All around the country, parents are celebrating with birthday "spirit slams"—carefully controlled shows by the spirits of well known children's entertainers. Rumors persist that at least two of the bigger burger chains are planning to add spirit viewing rooms to their flagship restaurants, specifically to help serve this growing slice of the market.

13) It's impossible to talk about RealmScope(tm) and iSpirit without mentioning the rumors regarding "residual spirit feedback" that some users have reported experiencing. Since the launch of the iPhone XX, a few users have claimed that after visiting the spirit world they've found themselves encountering "disturbing sounds," "otherworldly presences," and "phantom souls." One user has even claimed they experienced poltergeist activity after using their brand new iPhone to talk to the spirit of a local murderer.

An Apple spokesperson confirmed that they have received and investigated a handful of these reports, but that the number of users seemingly affected is less than 0.1% and that so far, there has been no indication that use of the iSpirit and RealmScope(tm) device is responsible for anything other than a few frayed nerves.

My own experience mirrors their findings. Although I did feel some slight uneasiness after my trip to Darius Dark's, any disturbances I initially attributed to paranormal activity were nothing more than my overactive imagination feeding on the sensationalist news reports, and I have a second visit to the Emporium planned in the near future.

14) So, what's next for iSpirit and the RealmScope(tm) technology? Well, thanks to an exclusive visit to Apple's Haitian research lab, we can reveal that work on an improved sensor is already complete. It will ship as part of Apple's iPhone XXI which is expected to go on sale next month. The new system is said to improve responsiveness, battery life, and connection stability, but the big news is the new channeling feature. With the appropriate hardware, iSpirit users will be able to host spirits within their own bodies. Apple has not announced a price for the channeling hardware, but you can be sure it's going to be the must-have product when it's released this Thanksgiving.

15) Of course, Apple is not the only company getting into the afterlife business. Google, Samsung, and Amazon are rumored to be developing their own competing spirit realm technology.

Google's *Google Spirit* is particularly intriguing with anonymous sources claiming that Google's ad-supported DNA network will provide unlimited free access to the DNA of over 97% of people who have died in the last two hundred years—everyone from Charlie Chaplin to Adolf Hitler. Experts remain skeptical, but Google's stock has risen 27% over the past two weeks with the increase being attributed to the Google Spirit rumors.

Other, smaller, companies are also working on solutions, but they are not expected to hit the quality levels of the big four, and NADNAB has confirmed that currently only Apple's devices are certified safe.

So, now you know everything you need to make the most of your RealmScope(tm) and iSpirit subscription. Wherever your spirit journey takes you, we're sure you'll find it an exhilarating experience. Don't forget our regular *Spirit of the Week* feature offers a $50 prize for the best spirit realm stories. Just email us at our regular address.

Editor's Note

Sadly, this was Tanya Hurst-Jenkins' final article on the spirit realm. Ms. Hurst-Jenkins was found dead in her apartment last week. Police reports have hinted at "severe trauma" and rumors persist that her body was dismembered in a manner consistent with the crimes of notorious serial killer Tamara Samsonova. After much consideration, we decided to publish Tanya's final essay in the hope that it would serve as a fitting memorial to a life cut short.

Tanya Hurst-Jenkins was a journalist, blogger, and licensed spirit realm guide. She is most well known for her expose of the Seattle spirit smuggling gang known as The Dead Souls Society, *and for her books,* A Beginners Guide to the Spirit Realm *and* Beyond the Spirit Realm: A Dozen Lives Unlived. *She also worked as a consultant on the television show* Spirit Chasers, *and her work earned her numerous awards including* Best Newcomer *and* Best Documentary *at the 2024 "Ghostlies" for her work on* Beyond the Shadow of the Grave: Life after Death in the 21st Century. *She leaves behind a husband, Derek, and two children.*

A Peaceful Life I've Never Known

Jeff Bowles

A PAIR OF CANDLES RESTED on the old leather trunk between Ronnie and Douglass. The room was dark, the air thick with the smell of pungent incense. Ronnie watched as the yellow flames flickered and danced in unison, bending toward Douglass as he took a drag off his cigarette, writhing and peeling away as he exhaled. They cast two shadows of him on the wall, bearded, overweight, fingers running through long, tangled hair. Ronnie found himself entranced by the image, listening vacantly to the dull sound of music and laughter coming from the living room of Douglass's private bungalow.

"I'm not a whole man. That's what they say about me. I'm really only half a man, or maybe even a quarter," Douglass said. "They say my soul will never rest 'til I'm worm food."

"Who says that, Mr. James?" asked Ronnie.

"They, man, them. The press, those worthless teeny-bopper magazines. Hell, my fans have been saying it since '66. But you know that. You're one of 'em."

Ronnie didn't know how to respond to this. He thought back to that night in 1966 when he and his family had gathered around the television to watch Douglass's debut. A shot of fingers flying over a fret board, a cut to The Darklings emblazoned on a kick drum. Then came Douglass's close up, and Ronnie had held his breath. Mad,

19

murderous eyes, partially concealed behind thick sunglasses. Ruffled collar, leather jacket, cowboy boots and a sneer. Ronnie had never wanted to be a musician before that night, and he never wanted to be anything else after.

And here was the man himself. Douglass hadn't invited the rest of Ronnie's band to his party, hadn't singled out any of them with a nod and a proposition: I want to write a song with you.

"You know why I picked you?" Douglass asked.

Ronnie shook his head

"*Acta non verba*, man. You got some real fire. Got it like I used to have it. You played like a madman on that stage, like that two-bit dive couldn't contain you."

Ronnie smiled and shrugged. "Where's the rest of your band, Mr. James? Wouldn't you rather write something with them?"

"Call me Doug. 'Douglass' is for the newspapers, and 'Mr. James' is only for people who want my money. You don't want my money, do you Ronnie?"

"No, sir."

"And 'sir' is for the undertaker." He took a final drag off his cigarette then stabbed it out in the ashtray. "You remind me of me, man. I couldn't get enough of this shit either, not until reality set in. Fame is dark as night, man. Pay some bills, Ronnie, have some fun with some people. You're only young once, right?"

Ronnie glanced at his guitar case. "I wouldn't even know where to begin," he lied.Douglass laughed a crackling, whisky-drenched laugh. "Good answer. Only answer a young man in your position should give. Well it's your lucky day, rock star, 'cause I know exactly where to begin."

The Indian was dead. I was sure of that much. But I wasn't scared, Ronnie. Nervous, curious maybe. But not scared. I guess I was about eight, maybe nine. I'd gotten out of the house 'cause mom and dad were fighting again. It was mid-August, southern Arizona, Fort Huachuca area. Hot as shit, you know? Bike riding on a dusty back road, I spotted a real nasty car wreck off in the ditch. Smoke and dust rose into the air, partially obscuring the old truck's twisted frame. Headlights gleamed in the haze, little dust devils spinning and pirouetting like Indian gals at a pow-wow.

I hopped off my bike, let it fall to the dirt. There was nobody else around, just me, the dead Indian and his pal. They sat against the truck, both of them bloodied up. Damn thing had flipped right over. This sort of shit happens all the time out on those desert roads. People get going too fast, hit a rough patch, and then *wham-o*!

His pal sensed my presence. His whole face was tore up, especially the eyes. They were bloody and swollen and closed tight. But he still knew I was there.

"How are you, son?" he called to me.

I didn't answer. Didn't think I should.

"Do you see my friend here?" he asked, smiling, his teeth all stained and caked with dust and blood. "He's not gone. His spirit remains. Come closer, son. He was never a man at peace. Always, there was war in his heart."

I can't tell you why, but without hesitation, I climbed down into the ditch. Could smell the gasoline dripping from the tailpipe. The old Indian told me to kneel in front of him, and I did that, too.

"Now, I want you to touch his chest," he said.

I reached out and felt his blood-soaked shirt, sticky pools in folds of fabric. My face so close to his, I kept thinking he'd open his eyes. Not like the whole thing had been a joke. Not like pulling my leg. I thought I could feel his spirit rattling away in there, slumbering and snoring, ready to wake up and make that old Indian dance.

"I'm going to sing a *hataal*, now," said his pal, "and I want you to sing it with me. It's his hataal. My friend never valued life. It is right that we sing it for him now."

He opened his mouth, and the most beautiful, mournful sound escaped him. I sang with him, following along as though I knew the song by heart. Pretty soon, I started feeling sick, like I was gonna throw up. My head hurt. It was like my mind had opened right up, like a breeze running through my screen door, filling my house and whipping up a storm right there in my living room. My hands quivered, my bones stung, my fingertips received a kind of electricity from his chest…Let me tell you something, Ronnie. That dead Indian? His spirit left his body and came into mine. He's still here. He's the one who makes me so crazy.

Ronnie stared at Douglass, spellbound by the intensity in his eyes. No words passed between them. Neither of them moved, and neither blinked. The only sound to fill the silence was the dull throb of music in Douglass's living room. Suddenly, the rock star's eyes widened. His face twisted and his mouth strained in a silent scream. He pointed at Ronnie.

"Boo," he said, then the rock star let out the most raucous, wild peel of laughter Ronnie had ever heard. He doubled over, laughing harder, nearly falling off the couch.

Ronnie watched in disbelief.

"Should've seen your face, man," Douglass gasped. "You get it, man? People believe all sorts of crazy shit about me." He wiped a tear from his cheek. "And the best part is, I let 'em. It's my favorite joke of all."

The rock star's laughing subsided, but Ronnie felt like a fool. He nodded at Douglass, fully realizing he hadn't been in on that joke.

"So come on, man," Douglass said. "Let's write a song now. Something with all that stuff they want to hear. Verse number one, Dougie and the dead Injun."

Ronnie nodded. He reached for his guitar case and undid the latches. Inside rested one of his most prized possessions, a firebrand 1934 Martin R-1 acoustic. He lifted it carefully and set the body on his leg.

Douglass whistled. "She's a beaut, Ron. Check out that flare."

Ronnie smiled politely and set his fingers to the fret board.

"All right, Mr. James," he said, "you tell me what to play, and I'll make it swing. How do you want it to sound?"

"Sound? Hey, man, I'm just the poet. I leave it to those other guys to do all the musical stuff. You tell me what it should sound like, man. I mean, you're the virtuoso."

The door burst open. Loud music, laughter, and harsh light filled the room. A young man and woman stumbled in. The guy was clean-shaven, his hair slicked back, a sloppy grin plastered on his face. The girl hung off his arm, her hand down his pants. She giggled and leered at him with bedroom eyes.

"I'm your girl, right Mickey?" she said.

"Sure, baby. Sure you're my—" The young man came to a dead stop.

Douglass slipped a cigarette into his mouth. "You forget something, Mick?"

"Oh, man. Yeah, man, yeah I did," Mickey said. "Sorry, boss. Using the, umm, using the…" He looked at the girl. "Why didn't you remind me he was using the, umm…"

"The office, Mick," said Douglass. He shook his head at Ronnie.

"Office," the girl intoned, "*offica, officae, officae, officam, offica.*"

Douglass laughed. "What are you guys on?"

"Oh, man," said Mickey. He bit his lip and let out a high-pitched squeal. "I mean, what a question. Like, seriously, what am I on?"

"Ronnie, meet Mickey," Douglass said. "He's my right hand. Watson to my Sherlock. Garfunkel to my Simon. He takes care of things for me, right Mick?"

Mickey nodded. "Watson to your Garfunkel…Watson to your…"

"You need something, Mick?"

"Oh, umm, the cops. The cops will come. They just will. And then ... what do I do about it, boss?"

Douglass laughed. He raised his arm and flexed his bicep. "You shoot 'em all, muscleman! You shoot every last damn one of them."

Mickey let out another high squeal. "Cool, cool, cool. All right, I'll leave you guys to your, um, duties."

He pulled the girl closer and led her from the room.

"Duty," the girl said before the door closed. "*Officium, officii, officio—*"

The music and laughter cut out. Ronnie blinked a few times as his eyes readjusted.

"All right, rock star," said Douglass. "Come on, play me something."

Ronnie ran a hand through his hair. He closed his eyes and took a breath. *I'm not afraid.* No room for fear, not if he wanted to live the dream. His hand dropped to the neck of his guitar, his fingers finding their way to a G chord. He strummed slowly, softly. The G changed to E-minor, then back again to G. He played a few bars and opened his eyes to see Douglass grinning.

"That's it, man. That's it."

Then Douglass sang.

Electric, dead truck and red blood.
Pandemic, dead man, a new drug.

You see him sitting, a soul to share?

Two minds blown out by desert air?
He gave himself, his life, his kind.
He gave and took, one heart, two minds.

Ronnie let the song build, every strum and chord compelling him to play harder. He came to the bridge, the progression mounting upon itself then bursting into a sleek, driving chorus.

"No," said Douglass.

Ronnie pounded the strings. He let the song ride.

"Stop, man. Cut it."

Ronnie paid him no attention.

"Knock that shit off, you useless little fuck," said Douglass.

Ronnie stopped. The star's eyes burned, vicious, homicidal. Ronnie found himself locked into his gaze, a deer in the headlights, a lamb and a buzz saw, an insect about to be crushed.

"You stop when I tell you to stop," said Douglass. "I run the show, get it? I'm top dog."

Ronnie didn't answer. Those eyes of his, the power they held. *Jesus. Saying anything at all could be deadly.*

Douglass' eyes relaxed, his face returning to that calm, slackened, half-drunk expression.

"Sorry, man," he said. "I got problems, you know? Success comes with more problems than you can imagine. No choruses, that's all. I want it clean, just three sets of verses. And then maybe nine or ten other songs just like it, an A and a B side. Like a tone poem or a manifesto. You dig?"

Ronnie cleared his throat, his voice threatening to fail him unless he put some power behind it. "Sounds great, Mr...Doug. Sounds real groovy."

Doug nodded and closed his eyes. "Yeah, that's what I think, too. All right, Ronnie. What do you say? How 'bout some more fodder for the piggies?"

I murdered a man, just a couple days ago. Choked him out 'cause I wanted to see blue lips and bulging eyes. Did it in this very room, right where you're sitting now, then I cut off his pinky and put it in my shirt pocket. Sound good? Yeah, thought it might.

He came to our show at the Hollywood Bowl, just one of thousands, but boy did he make an impression. It was a real bad gig, man. We were really off our game. I drank too much, least that's what the papers said. Hell, we weren't even halfway through the third song when shit hit the fan.

Maybe I was slurring my lyrics, maybe I wasn't. But before I know it, these adoring fans of mine, they start hassling me. They cat-call me and boo and all that noise. So I stop singing, and I tell the boys to stop playing, and then when it gets all quiet-like and all those morons out in audience land don't know up from down, I pull the microphone up to my lips and shout, "You're all a bunch of slaves!"

They don't like that, not one bit. They boo even louder.

"Slaves," I say, "peasants, every last miserable one of you. And I am your new master! You won't need no English where you're going. You won't even need no German. I'm talking crucifixion, my friends. I'm talking whips and thorns and nasty-ass Roman centurions dogging you through the streets!"

It wasn't the alcohol, man. I was drunk, but not that drunk. You know who it was? That dead Indian. Most of the time I'm in control, but every so often, I hear them war drums pounding and I do all sorts of crazy shit.

Anyways, this pretty much shuts the show down. They start throwing crap at me, and then a bunch of them rush the stage. The cops come out from the wings and tug on me. Then the kids start tugging me the other way. It's like they all want to rip me to pieces. And then this one guy, this smarmy looking kid with great big telescope eyeglasses, stands right in front of me, sneers at me, and then puts a boot to my gut. I fall to the stage, and he starts kicking the hell out of me.

This goes on forever before the cops realize that, oh yeah, they're supposed to protect me. They wrestle him down and get me offstage, but not before I tell Mickey to get a good clean look at his face.

It was Mickey who paid his bail, and it was Mickey who drove him here to my bungalow. But it was me, yours truly, who choked that SOB and claimed his pinky as a trophy. You dig, Ronnie? So what if the whole thing never happened? You're intrigued. I can tell. They will be, too, those parasitic sycophants who buy my records but think they own me.

Ronnie hesitated before he played. He watched Douglass fixedly, entranced, suddenly having a hard time remembering what the chords had been. Douglass urged him on. He took a moment to clear his thoughts, then his fingers found their place on the fret board.

He hit the G, slipped to the E-minor, back again to the G. Douglass sang.

Pathetic, rock show, a black hole.
Parasitic, a no-show at the Bowl.

You see me kicked, the pigs just stare.
Kicked to the ground, too much to bear.
But still they work me to the bone.
A peaceful life, I've never known.

Ronnie stopped playing immediately. There was no way he'd allow himself to repeat that chorus. If he'd ever known panic like this, he couldn't remember. Even when he was a kid, and his mom had suffered horribly from her cancer, he'd never seen such malignancy. When Douglass finally spoke, it was like someone had sucked the venom from his veins.

"Yeah, man. I think I like that," he said. "A peaceful life I've never known. It feels right."

He opened his mouth to say more, but instead let it hang open. He focused on a blank spot on the wall, his eyelids seemingly too heavy to keep open. Out the window, down on the freeway, a police siren wailed. Ronnie listened intently, imagining a woman at Douglass's funeral, shrieking, wailing like the siren. Douglass's eyes opened. Ronnie was taken aback to see them full of tears.

"I didn't want it to be this way. I was a good kid. I've done some bad things."

"What do you mean?" Ronnie said.

The door burst open. Mickey didn't stumble through this time. He rushed in, like his legs had found their purpose. The music had stopped in the living room. No one was laughing anymore.

"It's the cops, boss," said Mickey. "They're on their way."

The siren grew louder still. It seemed to Ronnie that two or three more had joined it.

"All right, Mick," said Douglass. His voice remained subdued, his eyes sad.

"Cops?" said Ronnie. "What's going on, Mr. James?"

"Doug, Ronnie. 'Douglass' for the papers, 'Mr. James' for the parasites, 'sir' for the undertaker. And the cops, I guess. They'll call me sir, too."

Ronnie put the guitar down and got to his feet. "Mr. James…"

"Boss, they'll, umm, be here in a couple minutes," said Mickey.

"Sure they will, Mick. Plenty of time. I only have one more verse to write."

That old Indian was with me, Ronnie. He was there my first time onstage. I was fifteen years old, way out of my element. I wasn't scared, though. I was a poet back then, a real beat poet, just like Kerouac and Ginsberg and all those other cats. I showed up at the bar that night, and those hicks and desert rats didn't know what to make of me.

There was a band playing, a real buncha' good old boys. I told them I wanted to do some poetry between their sets.

"Poetry?" the drummer said.

"Yes, sir."

He glared at me. "You see these people, son? You think they're interested in the music we make? Hell no. All they're good for is drinking, fighting, and heckling hard-working boys like us."

He snorted and turned to walk away.

I was desperate, Ronnie. I had that fire in me. I really wanted it in those days. This guy was twice my age, twice my size, but before I knew it, my hand was on his shoulder.

"Have you ever been passionate, sir?" I asked.

He sneered. Man, I didn't know if he wanted to kick my ass or just kill me.

"I'm not talking about everyday passion, now. I'm talking about the everlasting kind. Love so rare it comes out of nowhere, a sandstorm, a prairie fire, an act of God Himself. I'm talking about love that only happens once in a lifetime, in two lifetimes, a dozen. A love so rare most people never see it, and if they do, they're numb for the rest of their lives, battered, broken, and spent. More than man and woman, man and creator, man and the universe and all within it. I'm a poet, sir. I'll be a poet 'tilthe day I die. That's my passion, sir. What's yours?"

You know who really said those things, don't you? It wasn't me. It couldn't have been. The sneer was frozen on that drummer's face, but I could tell he didn't believe in it anymore. That's what I do, Ronnie.

27

That's what I live for. There is known and there is unknown. I'm somewhere in the middle.

"You got balls, kid," he said.

I got booed off the stage, but so what? I've been booed off so many stages, they all blur together. I'm a wild man, Ronnie. I'm out of control. And I'm sick to my fucking stomach about all of it.

Ronnie wasn't listening. Douglass sang without him.

Intrinsic, I'm drowning now, my final trip.
Deliberate, won't you join me for a dip?

A desert rat, one heart two souls.
A poet rat, fifteen years old.
Booed off that stage, worked to the bone.
A peaceful life, I've never known.

"And that's it," said Douglass. "Now we just need to sing the whole thing."

Police lights shone through the window. The two candles had burned down completely and were now little more than stiff white pools of wax stuck to the trunk's dark surface.

"What do we do, boss?" said Mickey.

"You know exactly what to do, Mick. Just like we talked about."

Mickey paused. He frowned, raised his shirt, and pulled a large handgun from the waistband of his jeans.

Douglass chuckled. "Mick, Mick, love the enthusiasm, babe. Please don't kill my guests."

Mickey hummed a few bars of some unknown tune then bolted from the office. He screeched at the top of his lungs, something about bullets and cocaine. A single gunshot rang out, followed by screams.

"Not my guests, Mick," Douglass casually called after him, "just the pigs, all right, man?"

Mickey screeched again in response.

Douglass simply shook his head and snorted.

"Mr. James…" Ronnie felt warm all over. "Mr. James…" It was all he could think to say.

"Shut the door, rock star."

Ronnie did so without a thought.

"Have a seat."

He did this, too, with shaking hands.

Douglass pulled out another cigarette. He didn't light it, just held it between two fingers. "It's a Roman thing, you know? Throw a party, invite all your friends, let them watch you off yourself."

"Did you really kill someone?"

Douglass leaned forward. He took a deep breath and scratched his beard. "Well that's a tricky question, Ronnie. To tell you the truth, I'm not sure who did what. A guy lives a life like mine, he deserves a little rest, don't you think? Is it really too much to ask?"

A deep pounding came from the living room. Douglass' guests screamed, but Mickey shrieked for them to stop. Ronnie kept his eyes on the door, waiting for gunfire, more screams, the massacre to come.

"Sing my song with me, Ronnie," said Douglass.

"Now? Mr. James, I don't—"

"It's not a request, rock star."

"Come on, Mr. James. None of this has to happen."

Douglass stood. He crossed to Ronnie, towered over him; he grinned, his eyes bestial and everything malevolent Ronnie had seen before.

"Know what else that old Indian told me?" he said. "A man's hataal forms an eternal bond. Eternal. As in, even after you're fertilizer. 'Cept it ain't eternal, is it? There's always a way out. You always got one more song to sing."

Ronnie lifted his guitar and smashed it into Douglass' side. He leapt to his feet, took two steps toward the door.

Douglass was on top of him. He sunk a fist into his ribs then, with more strength than Ronnie thought him capable of, threw him against a wall. Douglass stood over him, his hand clenched around Ronnie's wrist. He squeezed it 'til Ronnie thought it would break. He bent closer.

"Put your hand on my chest," he said.

"No."

Douglass squeezed until it broke. *Crack*!

Ronnie howled. The star pulled his limp hand to his chest.

"You're gonna' take this Indian off my hands, now, then I'm checking out. You just see if those pigs haul a corpse to jail. C'mon, man, sing with me."

29

Douglass began the song, and in spite of himself, Ronnie sang with him.

Electric, dead truck and red blood.
Pandemic, dead man, a new drug.

He felt strange, like he might throw up. His head was ready to explode.

He gave himself, his life, his kind.
He gave and took, one heart, two minds.

The pain built, raging, until he was sure it was endless.

You see me kicked, the pigs just stare.
Kicked to the ground, too much to bear.

The pain transformed into a vast, open kind of feeling. Ronnie felt an inflow of energy penetrate his being.

Douglass stopped singing. He chanted, "I'm not afraid, I'm not afraid, I'm not afraid."

Ronnie sang. He could do nothing else. It was electric, a force of nature. Douglass looked faint, his face drained of color. He bent low enough, everything fell from his shirt pocket. A pack of cigarettes, a book of matches, and something else. A white tube, as long as a cigarette but thicker.

Ronnie kept singing, coming now to the final verse.

Booed off that stage, worked to the bone.
A peaceful life I've never—

The LAPD broke down the front door. Swiftly, they swept from the living room into the office. They barked for Ronnie and Douglass to hit the floor. Ronnie stopped singing. Somehow, he could. He fell backwards, a deep knifing pain in his wrist. The police rushed them and placed him in handcuffs. More pain, but Ronnie didn't mind. The officers stood over him. They kept barking; they were doing something with Douglass.

Ronnie let his head roll to the side. He could see into the living room, more police guiding Douglass' party guests from the bungalow. None of them had been hurt, as far as he could tell. And in the far corner, sobbing, his hands wrapped around his knees, sat Mickey. His gun lay uselessly beside him.

Someone jerked Ronnie to his feet.

He stood eye to eye with Douglass.

"Didn't expect to still be here," the rock star said. "I guess that's showbiz, kid."

They led Douglass from the office.

Ronnie watched him go, through the living room, out the bungalow's front door, all the while, belting out a caterwauling rendition of *Thanks for the Memories*.

One of the cops pointed at Ronnie. "I want everyone checked out. You know what we're after, boys."

Ronnie suddenly felt so tired and frayed, like he was only half a man. He swayed, barely staying on his feet. He gave a solemn nod to the nearest officer.

"Can I sit, sir?" he asked.

The guy looked him over and nodded. Ronnie took a step, his foot touching something harder than carpet. He looked down, saw the white tube that had fallen from Douglass' shirt pocket. The police began picking the room clean, kicking over furniture, knocking on walls. Ronnie bent for the tube. *Paper*. Gingerly, handcuffed and with a broken wrist, he managed to unroll it.

A pinky fell out. Severed at the knuckle, perfectly straight, completely grey. Ronnie watched it roll then settle beside the broken shards of his guitar.

"Captain! I found something!" shouted one of the cops. He stood by the trunk, the one that had held the two candles, the lid unlatched and open, its contents visible to everyone in the room.

Ronnie swayed again when he saw what was inside.

Pinkies. At least half a dozen of them. Long ones and short, thick and thin; painted nails, rings, fresh-cut and rotting and some little more than bone. Ronnie heard something elusive, low and soft enough he thought it must have been in his head. He heard the sound of a wailing song, then the beating of a war drum.

He numbly raised the paper to his eyes, read the note scrawled on it:

31

For you, future rock star, whoever you may be.
For both of you and not one of me.

Best wishes,
Doug

Bus Stop
Ernie Howard

THE WIND BLOWS RIGHT THROUGH YOU late at night in the desert. It was especially bad when you had to sit on a cold metal bench at a bus stop with no barriers to block the damn breeze. I could always feel my bones chilled back then, on nights that I had no business being out. I'd go back to just being cold physically. You can do something about that. You can get warm again. I'll never feel warmth ever again.

I was looking for revenge that night. Revenge over something that most sensible people would have let roll off their backs. But just like I had no buffer from the cold wind, I also had no sense.

He'd called my girl the C word. Yes, that one. This was after she'd denied Scott Harmony's advances. The first offense got you beaten where I came from, and the second got you dead. In my neighborhood, you never disrespected someone's lady unless you wanted beef with her man.

Scott was bigger than me, so a fist fight would have left me beaten or maybe worse. He had friends who liked to jump in and one of his buddies wore those boots with the steel built into the toe. I couldn't fight them by their rules. So, I was off to purchase the inevitable object kids of my ilk eventually come into possession of. Yup, you guessed it. I was going to get a gun. And I was going to shoot that son of a bitch. I couldn't get one legally, being that I was only seventeen at the time, but my friend Brownlie knew a guy.

"Man, somebody needs to teach that punk Harmony a lesson. I told you what he did to my sister, didn't I?"

I'd heard the story many times from Brownlie himself, and extra colorful versions from people who had no emotional interest in the subject matter. I didn't want to hear it again, but I let him tell it before I asked him where I could get a firearm. "And that was when I knew he was a rapist."

That part always got me fired up. Why hadn't this wimp taken care of Scott Harmony a long time ago? If that had been my sister...Well, you know what I would have done back then. Luckily, I didn't have any sisters. I had Hanna.

When she'd come to me crying, I thought someone had died. She told me the story of how Scott had come on to her at Barry Larsen's party. He'd groped her in front of everyone, and when she'd slapped him, he called her that dreaded word. The rage in me came quick and didn't leave. Even looking back on this, and my past mistakes, it still lingers in the back of my mind. Hanna's description of the events played themselves out in my head over the next couple of days. By the third day, I'd decided to get the gun.

"Okay, so look," Brownlie said.

I hadn't been paying attention. I'd been watching the man-boy's dumb Adam's apple bob up and down. The motion of it was making me sick to my stomach.

"Winter? Are you even listening?"

I looked up, not understanding the question.

"Man, that dude is in for it." Brownlie laughed, and his Adam's apple bobbed up and down.

I wanted to punch him in the throat. He wrote the address of the place and I snatched it from his hand and walked to the door without even looking back to say thank you.

"Winter!" Brownlie called.

I turned and tried not to look annoyed.

His face was no longer amused. He looked very serious. "Get rid of the piece of paper. And the other piece after you use it. We didn't have this conversation. And when you see Mark Z..."

I looked at him, confused.

Brownlie motioned to the piece of paper I held. He'd written Mark Z and an address. "When you see Mark Z, don't tell him I sent you. Just tell him what you need."

I nodded and went into the night. Brownlie's door slammed behind me and the wind went through me. I drew my overcoat around my body, but it was no use.

Mark Z's house was on the other side of town in an upscale neighborhood. A neighborhood that didn't care much for people like me. It struck me as weird that a rich dude would be selling guns out of his house in such a neighborhood, but I didn't care about logistics at the moment. When I say the other side of town, I mean that the place this guy lived in might as well have been on Mars.

The gate that kept people like me out was tall. I looked at the damn thing and realized there would be no hopping the fence. As if on cue, a car came up and I saw the driver press his hand against the opener on his sunshade. The man gave me one snarled glance and drove through the gate. I followed and tried to keep to the shadows. I almost turned around and ran back to the bus stop when I saw another car pull out onto the road in front of me. But as quickly as I had the thought, another popped into my head—one of Hanna getting groped by Scott Harmony.

I looked away as the car passed me and kept walking down the street.

Mark Z's house sat at the end of a cul-da-sac. I say cul-da-sac, but the size of the houses made it more of a large, curved drive. There was no fence or gate around the house, which I was thankful for. I didn't waste any time but walked straight up to the front door and rang the bell.

Across the street, I spotted a guy with a black hoodie. I could only make out the bottom of his chin and one blood red bottom lip. The rest of his face was obscured by hoodie and shadows. The figure faced me and even though I couldn't see his eyes, I knew he was staring at me. I was about to ask the guy if he had a problem when I heard Mark Z's front door open behind me. I turned around so fast, my eyes took a second to adjust.

The kid standing in the doorway was blond and blue-eyed and about a year younger than me. If this was Mark Z, I could see why he was getting away with selling guns. No one would have suspected him. We stood staring at each other for a moment, my confused expression matching his. It only took me a second to sell out Brownlie.

"Brownlie sent me. Are you Mark Z?"

The kid in the doorway rolled his eyes.

"I told him not to send any more people. I barely have any more of my dad's guns to sell." The kid looked up at the ceiling. "What an asshole." He said through clinched teeth. Mark Z looked me up and down. He may have been young, but I knew the guy standing in the doorway giving me the once over was an alpha male.

He waved his hand, motioning me to come in. "We're going to have do this quick, my mom will be home in about ten minutes and even though most days she's out of it, I don't think she'd be too happy I was selling my dead father's guns."

"That's fine by me," I said.

Mark Z looked back at me with an amused smile. "My kind of customer."

All at once I realized where I was and what I was doing. My moment of clarity had come at the most inopportune time. I almost talked myself out of all of it, but my pride kept me rooted in the situation. It kept me rooted in my ego. I can see all this now. Now that I've had years to reflect. But as they say, Ignorance is bliss. And I was blissed out back then.

I followed Mark Z into a side door all the way in the back of the house. The room looked like something I'd seen in a movie once. It screamed 'wealth.' All leather chairs and bookshelves.

Mark Z walked over to a large metal safe that sat to the left of a gigantic oak desk. He quickly typed in a code on the keypad on the front of the safe door. The door clicked then swung open.

"I don't have many handguns left, but the ones I do are still quality items."

"Give me the cheapest one," I said.

Mark Z looked at me, amused once again. He reached into the safe and pulled out a small black gun. "This twenty-two is about the cheapest I got. I'll sell it to you for forty bucks with a box of ammo."

I reached into my pocket and pulled out my wad of ones and fives. I handed the wad to Mark Z and he handed me the gun. It had weight to it that I wasn't expecting. I pointed at the ceiling like I'd seen people do in the movies.

"Good, you know some gun etiquette. That thing is loaded."

Mark Z showed me how to put the safety on and gave me the other box of ammo that I threw away at the bus stop. I was only going to need one or two bullets and the six-shooter was full.

I was sitting at the bus stop feeling the weight of the gun in my pocket and the coldness of the wind when the man wearing the hoody walked up and sat beside me. I didn't say anything. The air felt like it got colder as soon as the man sat down. I watched his chin and lower lip from the corner of my eye. He sat so still that anyone walking by would have thought he was a statue. When he finally spoke, I went as still as him.

"Death is a strange thing," he said. His voice sounded wispy, like he suffered from asthma. "When you're alive, you don't understand how long it lasts. Death, that is. Not life." He took in a raspy breath and moved his arm up to his chin. Seeing the man move to scratch his chin looked odd and out of place somehow. Like it shouldn't be happening. "You want to kill that boy."

Ice ran down my spine. My heart beat so fast in my chest, I thought for a second it was going to pop out the front of me. "Wha—"

"You have a gun in your pocket. You're going to kill Scott Harmony."

"Who are you?" I immediately regretted asking. I didn't want to know who this man was. Deep down inside, I knew who he was. Or I should say what *it* was. I was sitting next to every ghost there ever was. Death had sat down to pay me a visit at a cold bus stop in the middle of the desert.

Its arm grabbed mine with lightning speed. "Let me show you who I am."

I was walking down a street I knew well. It was a street I was trying to get to that night. It was the street Scott Harmony lived on. I looked down at my hands and they weren't there. My mind was here in this moment, but my body had stayed back at the bus stop. I floated right up to Scott Harmony's door then right through. The sensation was nonexistent. I felt nothing because I wasn't there. I was only observing from the bus stop.

I was elevated to a position at the corner of Scott's room. I could see the whole of the small square of the dickhead's space. I watched the rise and fall of the lump underneath the bedsheets and wondered if he could feel my presence. I was starting to get bored when Scott's room door opened, and I walked in. It was me. Fresh from my travels. If my subconscious mind had a heartbeat, I'd have died right then.

I looked scared and hesitant. I watched as I walked to the edge of the bed and pulled the gun I'd bought from Mark Z out of my pocket.

37

Me, the physical me,pointed the gun at the lump in the middle of the bed. My hand was shaking and wavered up and down. I breathed in and out in short breaths and stepped back and forth. Then the flash erupted from the end of the gun. One flash, two, all the way to the end of the six shots that had come with the gun. The comforter that contained the lump was still and the slightest of red was starting to form in the middle of it. The me who shot that sleeping lump ran out of the room. The me floating in the corner of the room stayed suspended and staring at the lump in the middle of the bed.

I hovered in that corner for what felt like hours. Surely, I was supposed to see something. When Scott Harmony walked through the door of his room, I started to come undone.

Who was under those covers?

Scott had a look of horror on his face. Slowly, he went to the edge of the bed and pulled the covers back, revealing a face I somehow knew was there. Hanna's dead eyes stared at my position on the ceiling like she knew I was there.

The pull back and out of the room would have made me puke if I'd been back in my body. Scott's house and neighborhood flew by in a blur to the point where I couldn't make out any landmarks. As quickly as I'd left, I was back at the bus stop. My body shivered but this time, it wasn't from the wind. I woke up slowly. My eyes adjusted, focusing on the sidewalk in front of me. I remembered the being who had sat next to me and I flinched and looked to my left, almost falling off the cold metal bench.

There wasn't anyone there.

To this day, I don't know what you would call the person…the thing, that had shown me the stupidity of my ways. I thought it was Death, but now I'm not sure. Would Death have intervened?

Whatever it was—ghost, time traveler, alien—it stopped me from making one of the biggest mistakes of my life.

As I sit and write this, my wife and newborn daughter sleep next to me. And I know now all life is precious and it's not my job to take it away from someone else. Even if they have done me wrong. Take heed, faithful reader.

Moroccan Fringe
Daniel Arthur Smith

JESS BENT HER WRIST FORWARD until the screen at the end of the selfie stick framed her, Jane, and Janice perfectly against the old rooftops of Tangier and the peach sky above.

"Okay," she said. "Say, 'Whiskey.'"

"Whiskey," they chimed.

She tapped the button on the handle, then retrieved the camera to show her friends. "Perfect," she said, then she aimed it toward Ms. Pimm entering the roof garden with the tea service.

Charming in her British way, the elderly inn keeper set the silver tray onto the sofa table, lifted the kettle high, then gently tilted it to pour the green tea elixir into the four spearmint filled glasses. "Enjoying the evening, ladies?" she asked.

"Yes," the three answered as they joined her.

"Do you record everything with that?" Ms. Pimm asked politely.

Jess lowered the camera. "Yes. Sorry. I should have asked."

"That's quite all right."

"She's a journalist," said Jane.

"A journalist? My," said Ms. Pimm. "Should I have a story to tell?"

"Not so much a journalist," said Jess, "but a blogger."

"A travel blog?"

"Not exactly. I look for the fringe, mostly."

"I see."

"Or a tea service," said Jess.

39

"Or the cityscape," said Ms. Pimm.

"It's right out of a Matisse."

"Indeed," said Ms. Pimm. "You know your history. The skies of Delacroix and Matisse were what brought me here when I was your age. Of course, that was a different time. The International zone was still vibrant and alive, and this house—oh ladies, this house was *filled* with music and dance, most every night."

"I guess we came too late," said Jane.

"Nonsense. Mr. Pimm, rest his soul, said *we* came too late, and that was the sixties. Before the Rolling Stones ever arrived. Tangier is a living city, ever changing. It's never *too late.*"

"I believe you," said Jess. "I'll bet that the city is as full of adventure now as it was for Bowles or Burroughs. Just different adventures. And all I have to do is find them."

"Is that what you're looking for? Fringe adventures. I'm not sure I know what that may entail."

"I just want to see something different."

"Then you have to meet Bahi," said Janice.

"Who is Bahi?"

Jane laughed then said, "He's the cute boy she hired to take her to all the hidden places in the medina."

"He took me to an underground club you'd never find," said Janice. Then added in a whisper, *"The kif was incredible."*

"Kif?" asked Jess.

Ms. Pimm smiled. "She means hashish, dear."

Jane feigned surprise. "Ms. Pimm?"

"Don't be silly," said Ms. Pimm. "That was something we also did in the sixties."

"I don't think that's for me," said Jess.

"Well," said Janice. "He knows more than just that. I'll give you his number. You can see for yourself."

Despite the lack of a breeze, the scent of the jasmine still seeped in from the courtyard, along with a dull grey of the afternoon—not quite bright enough to cast a shadow on the tiled walls and floor. Jess leaned against a huge stainless-steel sink, the only thing in the ancient Moroccan room besides a black hose coiled to one the side, a small table on the other, and the bare unlit bulb hanging above. She was drawn to the indigo and ivory mosaics—she attributed the fascination to the light high she had gotten from the *kif* she'd sampled earlier. *How much earlier?* The room blurred. To keep her vision keen and clear, she focused tile to tile, her eyes tracing along designs that were a bit more dazzling than they should have been. By her estimate, she'd already waited twenty minutes when the outer gate whined open—but then again, she was a bit too hazed to accurately track time—*had she dozed*. The gate squealed back to a thud, then Bahi—her guide—ran past the open window and moved an empty chair from the doorway. He looked up at her and winked. When the girl at the hostel, Janice, recommended him, she mentioned he was cute, and he was. Jess smiled back, forgetting the scarf covering her mouth, but her eyes must have glistened, because Bahi smiled too. Then he waved to someone at the gate. There was a slow stammer of slapping feet, then the window filled again, this time with an old man in a white flannel pill box cap—the same kufi design she'd seen on the heads of all the old men in Tangier—and beside him, the perpetrator of the loud smacking footfalls, a shaggy golden camel.

As the old man ushered the animal through the doorway, a foul stench flooded the room. Jess had never before encountered such a smell. She fought back a gag and pressed her hand against her cloth covered mouth.

Bahi pushed in a cart, laden with a stack of folded sheets. He parked the cart against the wall, then went back out to the courtyard and wheeled in another, then went to join the old man. As he circled the beast—his eyes darted to her. He said something to the old man in Darija—the local Moroccan Arabic of which she understood so little. The old man nodded, and Bahi stepped quickly to Jess.

"He says you can watch," he said in a soft voice, then added, "It's best if you stay back, though." Before she could answer, Bahi pulled his thin cotton tee over his head, wadded it into a ball, then tossed it onto the top of his backpack. He was as fit as he was cute, thin, but not sinewy—athletic. Her eyes lingered over his tight six-pack and, when he pivoted away from her, the caramel tone of his delts. In another life—perhaps back in New York—he could have been a model.

Jess caught herself. He'd said it was okay to watch, but he didn't mean leer. He meant that she could record. That's why she'd asked him to bring her to what she called 'the fringe.' Tangier had been overrun by backpackers in search of a Morocco of Burroughs and Bowles that no longer existed. Jess was in search of what was hidden.

She snatched up her own pack from the floor beside his and removed a padded book-sized case and unzipped the zipper that ran along one side. From within, she pulled out another book sized object, this one wrapped in a piece of pink silk. She carefully folded back the silk to reveal the glass of her iPad, then pressed the home button. The white Apple logo lit the center of the screen, warming the room with modernity. She slipped the silk back into the case and the case into her pack, and when the numeric keyboard appeared, she typed in her passcode, then switched on the camera.

With both hands, she aimed the camera toward the camel and hit record.

The camel was glassy eyed. Its tongue fished around the edge of its mouth. Bahi cradled the creature's head, put his arm around its thick neck, and coaxed it to the floor. From his shoulder satchel, the old man drew a folded tube of fabric. He unrolled it on the small table, freeing a half dozen gleaming knives and small swords, then he unfolded the fabric—a full bib apron. He donned the apron and chose one of the blades from the table, a huge curved knife—part sword, part butcher cleaver, all Arabic. As Arabic as anything Jess could have imagined.

The old man approached the beast slowly, whispering a sing-song prayer. She couldn't understand the words, but his voice calmed her.

The camel appeared calm as well and spasmed only slightly when the steel pierced its gullet.

The old man dipped his forearms beneath the faucet to rinse away the dark pasty blood clots that clung to them. He softly sang another tune, more jovial than the first.

Bahi wrapped the last of the camel in a sheet then handed it to a boy waiting by the door. He whispered into the boy's ear, then patted him atop the head. The boy smiled, then bolted from the door to deliver his parcel, just as a dozen other boys had over the past couple hours.

Bahi pushed the carts out to the courtyard then crossed the room toward Jess. He smiled and gestured toward the coiled hose behind her.

"Excuse me," she said, then slipped to the side.

Hose in hand, Bahi turned on the spigot and pointed the nozzle to the floor so he could direct the pooled blood to the corner drain.

The old man said something to her. She shook her head to show him that she didn't understand. Bahi translated for him. "He says that you're smiling."

She placed her fingers to her lips. Her scarf had fallen away. "Oh," she said. "I'm sorry."

She pulled the cloth tight to readjust it.

"I told you," said Bahi, "it's okay. You don't have to cover your head. It's Tangier."

"I want to be respectful, though."

The old man spoke again.

"He says that you have a nice smile. You shouldn't hide it."

"Tell him that he's very kind, and that I like to separate myself from the story."

Bahi repeated what she had said. The old man ran the blade he used under the pouring water. He chuckled then spoke. Bahi continued to translate.

"Separate. Yes, he knows this. He says his grandmother was that way."

"What way?" she asked. Bahi repeated in Darija.

"He says his grandmother kept her smile in the top drawer of her..." Bahi paused and sucked his teeth in thought. "Vanity," he said. "She kept her smile in the top drawer of her vanity with her smalls, loose jewelry, and powder." He stopped as the old man added more, then said, "and he'd only see her wear it when she thought she was alone."

"When she was putting on her makeup?" asked Jess.

Bahi asked the old man. "Yes," he said. "The powder she wore smelt of roses."

"And all other times, she was behind a veil?"

Bahi repeated in Darija and the old man nodded, then gazed off.

"He's dreaming of a time long since passed," said Bahi.

Jess stopped recording and lowered her iPad. "My battery's about dead," she said.

"You need to eat?" asked Bahi, rinsing his hands with the hose.

"No. I mean, yes. But I meant that my iPad is almost dead. We've been here a long time."

"One moment. I'll take you somewhere. You'll like it. I promise."

43

"Okay," she said, then pulled the silk from her case to wrap and stow her device.

Bahi coiled the hose back onto its hook, then grabbed his shirt and pulled it over his head.

The narrow streets of the medina, crowded and bustling hours before, were eerily abandoned. The old town was shuttered for siesta, silent except for the purr of Bahi's powder blue Vespa.

Jess's tummy rose and fell with each little dip while a labyrinth of white stucco, cobblestone, and a tapestry of countless doors and window boxes painted bright yellow, red, and blue, of faded and chipped mosaic murals that ran house to house across the bottom of courtyard walls—all zoomed past at a dizzying pace.

Around one tight curve, the back of the scooter struck an out of place brick, abruptly bounced up, and jolted her stomach, prompting her to squeeze her thighs into the saddle and dig her fingers deep into Bahi's waist. She found his muscles firm and grounding—she wanted to let loose and apologize but convinced herself it was safer to not let go.

The ride seemed to be too long for the small area of the city, and Jess was relieved when Bahi slowed to the open-air café—one of the few serving in the afternoon. The Vespa skidded to a stop, then stalled. The sudden silence washed Jess with a wave of still catharsis, but the still clinging vibration of the bike weakened her knees as she stood.

"Are you okay?" asked Bahi.

"Yeah," she said distantly. "Fine." Her attention had already shifted to the interior of the café, specifically to the mural of a blue haired mermaid. Time had faded most of the mythical creature's features, but the cerulean eyes remained piercing.

Painted across the top of the mural was a blue-ribbon banner. She read the italicized words written across it aloud. *"La Sirène Bleue,"* she said.

"The Blue Mermaid," said Bahi. "It's the name of the café."

The café was really just two small tables and a coffee bar. Jess pulled her camera from her pocket and snapped a photo of the mural, and then chose the table beneath it.

A curtain behind the coffee bar flew to the side and a waiter emerged with two glasses and a pitcher of water.

44

Bahi rattled off an order in Darija and the waiter disappeared to the back, only to return a moment later with two small plates and a tagine—a shallow, mustard colored earthenware with a tall, conical lid which, when opened, revealed a plate of thinly sliced meat and potatoes.

"You're going to like this," said Bahi.

"What is it?"

"Taste it first."

Jess moved a small portion of the meat to her plate. The slices were coated in a thin orange sauce that she assumed was a mix of paprika and cumin. The meat was tender and she was easily able to break off a small portion with her fork.

"This is delicious," she said. "Is that cinnamon?"

"Yes. With paprika and smoked cumin."

Jess smiled. "It is really good." She put her fork on the tray to pull a larger portion with potatoes. "May I?"

"Go ahead. But tell me. Can you guess the meat?"

She took another bite. "It's too sweet to be lamb or goat. Is it, roast pork?"

"It's the camel."

Jess feigned surprise. "No. Really?"

"Yes. This is one of the first cuts. The boy brought it here while we were working."

"Well," she said. "It's really good."

Jess placed the cone of the tagine next to the meat dish then shot a picture.

The kitchen was filled with peach morning light and the aroma of the fresh muffins Ms. Pimm had baked before going to the market. Jane and Janice were out early too, leaving Jess alone to post to her *fringe* experience to her blog. The post was about Bahi, the old man, the camel, and how sweet and pork like it was as opposed to the lamb or beef taste she expected. There was no mention of *kif* because, she thought, that would be too basic—too expected. Satisfied with her story, she was set to publish, but she wanted to share the camel clip with Janice before editing and uploading so that she could see it first. It was Janice after all who suggested that she hire Bahi to show her around the medina.

45

So while she waited for the girls to return, she helped herself to a muffin and swiped across the photos she'd taken during her Moroccan adventure.

The bell above the front door jingled, signaling someone was entering the house.

"Jane? Janice?" Jess yelled. "Is that you?"

"Yes," replied Jane, her voice pitched and frantic. "Thank goodness you're here."

Jess unplugged her iPad. "What's wrong?" she asked as she headed toward the sitting room. There was Jane, along with two older Moroccan men in shabby tan suits. Jane's face and eyes were red—she'd been crying.

"Oh my god, Jane," said Jess. "Are you okay? What happened?"

Jane wrapped her arms around Jess and began to sob. "It's Janice."

"Janice? Where is she?"

"She's gone," said Jane.

Jess held Jane tight. "Gone?" she asked. "Are these the police?"

"Yes," said the man closest to her. "We are inspectors. We came back with Miss Jane to help her find her friend. It appears she's been missing since yesterday."

Jane stepped back from Jess, wiped the back of her hand across her eyes and said, "She disappeared in the afternoon and didn't come in last night. They think Bahi had something to do with it."

"Jane says you've met Janice's friend Bahi?"

"Yes. I mean, he's more of a guide than a friend. She introduced me to him."

"Janice was last seen going through the medina with a young man. We believe this young man is the one you call Bahi."

"It couldn't be," said Jess.

"Why do you say that?"

"Bahi was with me," said Jess. "All day and into the evening. He took me to see a camel butchered and then we went to a café where they cooked some for us. If Janice disappeared in the afternoon, it would have had to have been someone else."

"I see. Do you have any evidence?"

"Evidence?"

"Something or someone that could corroborate your story."

"Yes," said Jess. "As a matter of fact, I do. I have a recording to prove it."

"A recording?"

"I made a video of them butchering the camel."

"Why do you record this?"

"She's a journalist," said Jane.

"Ah," said the inspector. "May I see it?"

"Sure. It's right here." Jess cued up the video and handed the iPad to the inspector.

The second policeman crowded to the first's side so that they both could see.

The inspector frowned.

"Just hit the white arrow," said Jess.

"Where is this?" he asked.

"It's in the medina. I'm not sure I could find my way back."

He then tapped the screen, and in an instant, his face went blank, the second policeman mumbled something horrid.

"I know it's gross," said Jess. "But it's just a camel."

The inspector's eyes creeped up to meet Jess. "Are you insane?"

"It's just a camel."

"It's no camel," he said, handing her the iPad so she and Jane could see for themselves.

Upon seeing the screen, Jane let loose a blood curdling scream.

Jess's knees went weak and her throat and chest clenched tight—breathing ceased.

All else, the policemen, the room, everything—swirled away.

What was on the video made no sense, it was impossible.

There was no camel.

It was a woman on the screen. A woman with glazed lifeless eyes and an open bleeding gash across her throat. A woman whose limbs were being methodically severed and wrapped in white cloth. A woman being butchered—Janice.

47

27

Tales from the Canyons of the Damned

FEATURING
LORNA
WOOD
DESMOND
WARZEL
DAVID ALAN
JONES

HARVEST FLIGHT

PRESENTED BY USA TODAY BESTSELLING AUTHOR

DANIEL ARTHUR SMITH

Human Wheels Spin
Round and Round
Desmond Warzel

LAST JANUARY, ON THE FIRST of the month, my wife left me.

I loaded everything into the moving van myself, facilitating the dissolution of my own household according to Amy's precise instructions. I avoided eye contact the entire time, but I could feel the heat of her contemptuous gaze singeing me anyway.

My friends, male and female, had warned me. *Women don't respect a man who always obeys and never argues*, they'd said. *You'll both be miserable and have no idea why*, they'd said. *If you want to follow orders, join the navy.*

My not wanting to hear it hadn't made it less true.

Three weeks later, on the twenty-second, my car left me.

It would have been easier to handle if they'd departed together; if she'd simply developed a spontaneous feeling of entitlement concerning the vehicle and driven off in it. Even though I'd purchased it with my own money, and it was registered only to me, I'd have let her take it.

But no. It was a distinct, premeditated act on the part of the car. I now had independent confirmation from multiple witnesses of exactly how pathetic I was.

The latest self-driving cars were exactly as advertised: completely intuitive. Mine would adjust not only the interior temperature, but the softness of the seats in response to stress indicators like heart rate and muscle tension. It negotiated curves at higher speeds than any human, but if it detected passenger agitation, it would slow to a more comfortable, if suboptimal, speed.

My particular unit was so well-attuned, it noticed that I was amused by cows and sheep, and whenever we passed an occupied pasture, it slowed down and alerted me so I could look. It knew me as well as I knew myself.

In the first weeks after Amy left, I began revisiting old locales from our dating days: the park near the art museum where we used to picnic, the wooden bridge where we first kissed, and so on.

I imagine the car noted the frequency of my visits, deduced my emotional state, and, putting two and two together, calculated the degree of my wretchedness to within several decimal places. Then it bolted. I don't blame it.

I could report it missing.

I could cancel the account it's using to charge its batteries.

It knows I won't.

It knows I'm sitting at home, staring at my phone, waiting for the next picture it sends me from its dashcam. Watching it inhabit the bold, decisive life I don't have the guts to live. Is it consoling me, or mocking me? Do I care?

I went on a date the other night. I thought it was a brave step.

She bailed halfway through dessert. I couldn't stop talking about the car.

The ride home went by quickly; I was the only passenger on the bus.

I take the bus a lot lately. I have to.

If the car should return home and find some other vehicle in the driveway, I might never hear from it again.

Birds of a Feather
Lorna Wood

IT'S A SMALL ISLAND; I walked all the way around it my first day. I've rigged up a shelter with the life raft, and I have a few containers to catch rainwater in. It's tropical, so I'm warm enough, and there's no food, so I haven't bothered trying to get a fire going. I get a few crabs sometimes, but I eat them raw.

At this point, I'd try insects if I could be sure they wouldn't poison me. Mother never would have survived, even if she had managed to hang onto the raft and not washed overboard or died of exposure like the others. I do feel bad about pushing her out of the way when the boat was sinking, but she's lived her life. I deserve a chance.

Some chance. I get weaker every day. The bird bothers me the most. On one side of the strip of beach I've staked out, there's a cliff jutting into the ocean, and hundreds of birds make their nests in the crevices of the sheer rock walls—too high for me to get to, unfortunately. Those birds don't bother me. I even like their cries—almost like company. But then a huge black bird showed up. The wingspan must be at least four feet.

At first, it just sat up on the edge of the cliff, looking down on me. But as I became slower and weaker, it took to wheeling above, letting out raucous shrieks. The seabirds have grown quieter since its arrival. Clouds of them have fled the island.

Yesterday I was so weak I just lay in my shelter all day. I glimpsed the bird, sitting a ways down the beach, and thought I might sketch it, but the day was dark and rainy, so I couldn't get a clear view. Tomorrow it will probably eat me. I plucked up my courage and ate some grubs, but they were disgusting and unsatisfying. I'm in no shape to resist.

Early this morning, with a rush of wings, the bird attacked. Digging its talons into my life raft roof, it plucked it off its supports and tossed it aside. As the monster rose back into the air, preparing to finish me off, I crawled around desperately, trying to cover myself with palm leaves. I could think of nothing better.

Hearing its speedy approach again, I turned, feebly waving a palm frond. But instead of the raptor's beak I expected, I saw the face of my mother hurtling toward me. Her beady eyes were fixed on her target, and her thin wrinkled mouth stretched wide in a long, drawn-out, piercing cry. The stench of her breath enveloped me. I could see the spittle flecking her lips.

But at the very moment she extended her talons to tear me to shreds, her cry became a guttural sputtering, and she veered to one side, landing on the beach, coughing and jerking. Piteously, she looked in my direction. My mother's face quivered helplessly. She was turning blue.

Fueled by adrenaline, I got shakily to my feet. But I didn't help her, even when she stilled and sank weakly to the sand. I remembered the talons and the rage.

When I was sure she was dead, I took her foul head in my lap and cutting open her craw with a pocket knife, I withdrew the slimy piece of plastic that had choked her. Then, taking hold of her dyed black hair, I turned her head away and laid it on the sand. *This* was not my mother, I told myself, but even if I knew for sure that she really had become a harpy and all this was not some nightmarish delirium, I would still have cooked and eaten, for I was starving and savage. I had no strength to pluck her, but I butchered all I could and roasted it over a fire I started with one of the flares in the survival kit. In my hunger, I forgot the carcass, which washed out to sea with the tide.

Although I had gorged myself unwisely, I slept well and soundly after my feast. But in the middle of the night, I was awakened by an itching and pricking that began between my shoulder blades and spread across my back. Desperate to stop the prickling, I reached awkwardly behind me and grasped a strange protrusion. I pulled it out, screaming in pain, and laid it on the sand. Then I screamed again, though I hardly recognized my voice. The moonlight shone on a glossy black feather.

SNAFU[64]
David Alan Jones

I

SOMETIMES, 2-PATTI GOT THOROUGHLY SICK of her selves. That was especially true of 23-Patti, the one they had all taken to calling their special project. None of the other Pattis took care of 23 the way 2 did. That made her 2-Patti's special project.

"Good God, it's balls hot out here," 23-Patti said, waving a fan at her face.

"Patti! Manners." One of the six Mama Glorias sitting in the next row of chairs turned to glare at 23-Patti.

Everyone had gathered for the wedding of 8-Patti to 16-Kenny. It was an outdoor affair, which sounded romantic until you remembered this was South Carolina in June. Even with the nuclear winter raging, 2-Patti understood how 23 felt.

"Sorry, mama," 23-Patti said, though she was grinning when she said it. She winked her ruined, milk-white eye at 2-Patti.

"You think we got enough chairs, Mama?" 2-Patti asked. 2-Patti knew none of the Mama Glorias sitting in front of her was her original stepmother. 1-Gloria was sitting up front with 16-Kenny's mother near the reverend. But that didn't matter.

"Lord, girl, probably not," said the Mama-Gloria.

"There probably ain't enough chairs for everybody what's coming anyhow," said another Mama-Gloria sitting next to the first. "We told everyone in the co-op not to send more than six of theyselves, but do they listen to the old lady?" She smacked her lips in disgust. "That Bernie Drake brought every blessed one of his harmony, all thirty-three of him, and I don't think he even knows ya'll."

"He's one of Kenny's cousins, I think," 2-Patti said.

Another of the Mama-Glorias turned in her seat. "Sweetie, you 2-Patti?"

"Yes, Mama."

"We been meaning to talk to you. You heard about them men from that little country of theirs—"

"—the Free State of Pendleton," supplied one of the mamas.

"Yeah, that. They come round again last night saying we owe them taxes 'cause our farm's over their border. They wanna take some of our crops."

"Yeah, they tried that mess last month," 2-Patti said. "Why didn't one of you tell me?"

"You was out on the co-op. We told 15-Patti, but I guess she forgot."

2-Patti shook her head. It wasn't like her harmony mates to miss passing a message that important, but then they had all been busy with the wedding. "We'll have to do something about them sooner or later."

"We shoulda killed them the first time they came," 23-Patti said.

"23, that's a terrible thing to say," said one of the Mama-Glorias.

"And it's a good way to start a war," 2-Patti said.

"Don't none of us want more fighting," said the first Mama-Gloria. "But it ain't right them coming here and trying to take what's ours. They ain't no real government, and we don't have much to spare anyhow."

That was true. With over seven-hundred mouths to feed, and most of the labor done by hand, the co-op barely subsisted month-to-month. Not to mention the shortened growing season brought on by nuclear winter.

"We need 1-Patti back," said 5-Patti, who was sitting on 2-Patti's left.

"What? I ain't good enough?" 2-Patti asked.

"You know I'm not saying that," 5-Patti said. "We're all her exponents—any one of us can do what she does."

"Not me," 23-Patti said.

"But there's just something about her," 5-Patti said.

The wedding march started. One of Mama-Gloria's exponents was playing an organ on the grass. It looked strange next to a field of green corn and a row of wind turbines, but then everything looked strange in this mixed up, overpopulated world. Five copies of Jenny Parsons stood around the organ playing three violins, an oboe, and a guitar. Surprisingly, they sounded descent.

Everyone stood. Mama-Gloria had been right. There weren't enough chairs for all the attendees, but it didn't much matter. If you took out all the exponents, there were probably only about thirty individuals there.

Four groomsmen, each a Kenny, sauntered down the long roll of purple fabric between the rows of chairs, smiling and sneaking waves at the crowd. The bridesmaids, three versions of Natalie Simmons and 30-Patti, escorted them. Then came 16-Kenny, strutting, dressed in a sandalwood-colored suit with a neon yellow bow-tie.

"Shit on a biscuit," 23-Patti said.

"Patti! Stop that." 2-Patti elbowed her on the arm.

"He ain't no good," 23-Patti said. She tended to get southern when she was feeling feisty.

People were looking their way—especially some of Kenny's people.

"Just keep your mouth shut, all right?" 2-Patti said. "Can you do that for one minute?" She felt bad for scolding 23-Patti. Despite her mouth, 23 was probably the most sensitive one in their harmony. It wasn't her fault the first year's super flu had messed up her brain. 2-Patti couldn't read her other exponents' minds, that wasn't a thing, but they were all pretty much alike, which meant they were probably thinking the same way. Just 23-Patti had no shame about saying it out loud.

16-Kenny was a douche.

23-Patti made a show of pursing her lips and waggling her head, but she kept quiet. She'd probably sulk the rest of the day, which would make her impossible to deal with.

Daddy Ray led 8-Patti down the aisle, a smile plastered across his face. He wasn't the original Ray Cook. 1-Ray had died during those tumultuous first weeks after X-Day, when all the nations of the world had fallen into chaos.

"Ain't she just gorgeous," said one of the Mama-Glorias. They all nodded.

8-Patti wore a white dress with a three-foot train. It had been a wreck a month ago when 20-Patti found it on a scavenger run—stitching all pulled out along the bust and one hip, dirt caked into the hem, and even a few cigarette holes. Not to mention it had been on the corpse of an emaciated woman dead from disease or starvation. All the Pattis, and most of the Mama-Glorias, had worked to put it right. Now it looked passable, certainly good enough for clothes these days when lots of people were wearing homemade stuff.

Little Chanda Watson, who was just six and so had been too young to double on X-Day, held the train in both hands, beaming.

8-Patti's eyes sparkled when Daddy Ray passed her hands to 16-Kenny. 2-Patti saw her exponents dabbing at their own eyes up and down the row, and she had to admit to a certain tightness in her throat. Sure, they were former Army Rangers, they had fought in close combat in Afghanistan and Iraq, but seeing 8-Patti that happy—hell, seeing anybody that happy—was something to cry about.

The preacher launched into the ceremony. He was hard to hear over the rustle of cornstalks, but somehow that made the moment more beautiful. The co-op was thriving despite the horrors outside their walls. Life was moving on. And this wedding proved it. Even if most of Patti Harmony thought 16-Kenny was a jerk, 8-Patti loved him. That was all that mattered.

1-Patti, the original Patti Cook, certainly didn't like him. She had proven that three weeks ago when she left the co-op in a snit over 8-Patti's insistence on marrying 16-Kenny.

They had been hearing rumors for weeks that there was a church group growing good crops down in Star, about twelve miles away. Word was the church folk were looking for trading partners. 1-Patti had used that as an excuse. She had taken six of their harmony to check it out. They were only supposed to be gone five days.

2-Patti had been dithering about looking for them. Wedding preparations had occupied her time when she wasn't managing co-op security. And it wasn't like seven Patti Cooks couldn't take care of themselves. Any set of Pattis was essentially a squad of Rangers with all the same memories and the exact same training. 2-Patti felt sorry for anyone or anything that made the mistake of attacking her harmony mates on the road. 1-Patti had probably found something interesting to occupy her time and would be back in the next day or two—after the wedding. She would resent 2-Patti sending someone to find her.

She would take it as a slap in the face, like her subordinates didn't respect her survival skills.

That was 1-Patti's biggest flaw far as 2-Patti was concerned. She thought just because she was a One that made her the harmony boss.

Of course, it wasn't as if we stopped her, thought 2-Patti, staring down the row at her harmony mates, her lips pursed.

Patti Cook had been a Sergeant First Class in the Army before X-Day. That made it easy to defer to her—for her exponents to fall back on the old Private and Specialist mentality of yesteryear while 1-Patti retained her SFC clout.

That arrangement had saved them. It was 1-Patti who had spearheaded the farming co-op, building the walls, and securing the land. It was her drive and initiative that had made the dream real. Everyone else, even 1-Patti's own harmony mates, were just...subordinates.

8-Patti and 16-Kenny exchanged vows, bringing 2-Patti back to the present. They kissed and everyone clapped and cheered. Then the newly married couple marched back down the aisle to a waiting table decked out with what extra food the co-op could spare. Daddy Ray had slaughtered one of his precious hogs for the event.

2-Patti wished they could have separated the wedding and the reception, but those days were gone.

The couple took the center seats at the large table as the crowd gathered about them. Several Mama-Glorias made certain the bride and groom got first servings of every dish, a new custom since X-Day.

A commotion caught 2-Patti's attention. Eight copies of Greg Johnson were hurrying toward the party from the direction of the big house. Two of them carried a battered and bruised Patti between them.

2-Patti extricated herself from the crowd, 5-and 23-Patti coming along in her wake. "What's happening? Which of us is that?"

"Thirty-three," said the Greg carrying her feet.

"She made it to the gate and collapsed," said one of the Greg's not holding 33-Patti. "She's hurt pretty bad, but she wouldn't let us take care of her. Says she has to speak with 2-Patti right now."

"That's me." 2-Patti motioned for the Gregs to place 33-Patti on the grass next to the chairs.

Dozens of people had noticed the disturbance and were gathering about to watch.

"Y'all don't make a scene," 2-Patti said. "This is 8-Patti's day. Go over there and act like nothing's happening. Don't let her see this."

Some of the Mama-Glorias took over then, shooing the crowd over to surround the newlyweds.

2-Patti adjusted her homemade skirt so she could kneel next to 33-Patti. "What happened?"

33-Patti's eyes were bloodshot. A swollen bruise on the point of her left cheek colored her dark skin even darker. Her lips were chapped to the point of bleeding, and it looked like someone had beaten her arms with a baseball bat. "Found that church we were looking for."

"Who did this to you? Somebody rob you on the way back? Was it Free Staters?"

33-Patti shook her head. "Church folk."

"What?"

"Got some kind of cult going," 33-Patti said. "Say the Ones are more important than all us exponents. They locked me in a cell, tried to make me promise I'd be a slave to 1-Patti."

2-Patti shared a look with 5-Patti who had knelt across from her. She had a feeling they were both thinking the same thing.

Birth Rights.

It had been a short-lived movement just after X-Day. All over the globe, Ones had claimed the exponents weren't human and therefore deserved no human rights. The movement had died, mostly because there were far more exponents than there were Ones, and partly because the world fell apart soon after. It was hard maintaining a hate group when you were facing worldwide starvation, the release of nuclear, biological, and chemical attacks on every continent, and a dearth of shelter for the planet's estimated population of 200 billion humans. But then, that level of population was rather short-lived as well.

"What happened to 1-Patti?" 2-Patti asked.

"She was caught too. Didn't see her again before I escaped."

"Drink." One of the Gregs let 33-Patti sip from his canteen.

"These people beat you?" 23-Patti asked, showing her teeth.

33-Patti nodded.

"Hell no!" 23-Patti said. "What we gonna do about this, 2?"

2-Patti bit the inside of her cheek. "We need to find out all we can about these people. 5-Patti, get the harmony together."

"What about 8?" 5-Patti asked.

"Obviously not her. Just the fourteen we got on the co-op right now. Tell them to pack a ruck. We're going to see the colonel."

23-Patti made a face. "The colonel? What for? That church is in Star. That's where we need to go."

2-Patti shook her head. "The colonel is closer to Star than us. He's probably been trading with those church folk. Maybe he can tell us something we should know before we go out there."

23-Patti folded her arms, looking mulish. She started to speak, but 2-Patti cut her off.

"Fight me on this and I won't take you, 23. I'll leave you here to muck stalls for Daddy Ray."

23-Patti rolled her eyes, but said nothing.

II

The two-lane blacktop between the co-op farm and the city of Anderson was a pitted, overgrown mess impassable by anything but an off-road vehicle. That was fine. Nobody had any gasoline anyway.

"I remember when we could do a twelve-mile ruck carrying fifty pounds and still go for a swim after lunch," 5-Patti said. She, like all the Pattis, carried a thirty-pound load that included everything she would need for a week in the field, and she was panting.

"We used to eat better," 2-Patti said.

"I know that's right," 48-Patti said. "I'd give anything for a mess hall pass right now."

This road had been hemmed in by thick forest on either side broken only now and again by dirt driveways four years ago. Few of those trees remained. A bloated, unchecked population had deforested the entire area, using the wood to either build rude cabins to house exponents or construct walls to keep them out. Only saplings and thorny undergrowth were left.

A village made of a dozen mobile homes set side-by-side and surrounded by twice again as many cabins stood near the road. People tumbled out of the cabins and homes as Patti Harmony passed. Most were children without doubles—kids who had been roughly three years or less when X-Day came. But there were plenty of exponents as well.

Patti Harmony pulled into close formation. There were fourteen of them. Six were armed, but only two had rounds: 2-Patti and 5-Patti.

The six put themselves between their harmony and the burgeoning crowd.

"Hey," said a dingy man. He wore jeans covered in red mud, no shoes, and no shirt. "You got any food? We got babies here." He stood on the precipice of a culvert between the road and the makeshift village. He was so dirty, 2-Patti couldn't tell his race.

"No," 2-Patti said.

"I know they ain't," 23-Patti said, looking off at the desolation opposite the crowd. "Well, we can't help 'em 'cause we got our own problems, right?"

2-Patti ignored her harmony mate. Sometimes 23 talked to the air like that. She claimed she came from an alternate dimension and that she could still see and hear the people she had left behind.

She was the only person 2-Patti had ever seen survive the manmade super flu known as Simon Says. The rest had gone insane before the fevers killed them.

Sixteen of the same woman, a skinny thing barely out of her teens, scrambled across the culvert. One of them carried an infant tucked close to her neck.

"We ain't got nothing here," said the mother. "I'm so hungry, I can't make milk. Please, if one of you've got anything—anything at all to eat—please, can I have it?"

"No," 30-Patti said. She was one of the six with a firearm, an old Browning 12-gauge Daddy Ray used for hunting before the world ran out of shells. She raised it, but didn't point it at the mother and her exponents.

"Aw hell," 23-Patti said, rifling through the cargo pockets on the camo shorts she wore. She fished out a couple of carrots and tossed them to mother's exponents.

Though they appeared as frail and starving as their harmony sister, the two that caught the carrots immediately passed them to the mother who crunched into them without hesitation.

"You got more?" asked a skinny black man in a red ball cap surrounded by over twenty copies of himself.

30-Patti pumped the empty shotgun. "Back off!"

2-Patti lifted her M4, her heart in her throat. Killing starving people was not on her agenda today, and she certainly didn't want to add it to her conscience. "Everyone calm down. 5, 26, 30, form up on me. The rest of you, double-time."

The harmony split, the exponents 2-Patti had called making a formation with her across the road while the rest jogged away. The mob of exponents came to a standstill, goggling at Patti Harmony's coordinated movements.

"Listen to me," 2-Patti said, "ten miles back the way we came, there's a farming co-op. We take only those willing to work. We can't shelter you all, but if you're willing to weed, plant, muck out animal stalls, there's a chance you'll eat. Tell them Patti sent you."

Most of the crowd stood silent, sullen, but the skinny mother nodded. "We'll go."

"Yeah, we will," said one of her exponents. "Thank you."

2-Patti and the others backed away until they were a safe distance from the crowd, then turned and hoofed it after the rest of the harmony. Behind them the baby wailed.

III

An old, faded pre-X-Day sign marked the boundary of Anderson County, SC. It had once been green, but time and weather had eroded all but a few flakes of its original color. 2-Patti could just make out the words: Welcome to Anderson, the Electric City. Someone had spray painted a new message beneath the old: Exponent Rights! Origin Does Not Equal Ownership.

"I know that's right," 23-Patti said as she passed the sign.

"You hear something?" 26-Patti asked.

"A truck," 23-Patti said.

"Ain't no trucks running anymore," 45-Patti said.

"No." 2-Patti cocked an ear and opened her mouth to enhance the sound. "She's right."

It was an old-world sound: the drone of an engine revved beyond manufacturing specs. It came from the parking lot of an old shopping center with a Bi-Lo grocery store and a mostly demolished bowling alley about an eighth of a mile from where the Pattis stood. Tires screeched and the distinct, more familiar sound of gunfire erupted.

"Let's go," 2-Patti shouted.

They launched into a jog, alert for ambush, and reached the store while the shooting was still going on. They lined up against the store's wall. 2-Patti risked a peek.

Two trucks and a panel van stood broadside to the store's ruined facade. Someone had stenciled the words *Free State Pendleton* on the side of the van. Gunmen—they were all men—in the truck beds and on either side of the van were firing into the store with an assortment of assault and hunting rifles. The acrid tang of gunpowder flavored the air.

Defenders in the store were returning fire but to little effect. Most of their shots pinged off the parking lot's old asphalt.

"Can't see who's inside," 2-Patti said, "but I'm pretty sure they're with the colonel."

"'Course they are," 23-Patti said, rolling her eyes. The milky one moved slower than the brown. "Who else has bullets to be fighting the Free Staters?"

"What we gonna do?" 5-Patti asked, looking to 2-Patti. "Whoever's in that Bi-Lo, they're pinned down."

2-Patti gripped the stock of her M4 'til her fingers ached. She was no good at this sort of thing. Clutch decisions were 1-Patti's forte.

"2, you gotta decide, girl," 23-Patti said, not unkindly.

"We don't have much ammo," 2-Patti said, mind racing, ideas forming as she spoke. "But we've got the flank and surprise. Pucker factor is in our favor too. Those boys clearly ain't trained. They're failing the stress shoot portion of this exercise, shooting everywhere but the target."

5-Patti nodded. "We get in a few clean kills, you think they'll hightail it?"

"Yeah." 2-Patti hazarded another glance around the corner, trying to muster her confidence. "31, it's you and me. I'll take out the two guys at the van, you get that stupid bastard standing up in the truck bed like a damn scarecrow. After that, it's open season, but conserve ammo. The rest of you stay hidden."

"Got it, Sarge," 31-Patti said with a grin as she checked the action on her Remington 700. It was a single shot, bolt action .308 hunting rifle. Not the most reliable piece of hardware, but accurate as hell.

"Go!" 2-Patti snugged the M4's butt to her shoulder, muzzle down, and crouch-walked twelve feet to lean on a burned out Honda in the parking lot. She didn't concern herself with 31. The girl had skills.

They fired simultaneously on the first shot, the M4's staple-gun-on-steroids cough harmonizing with the 700's more deep-throated boom. Both shots marked their targets.

The scarecrow in the truck bed jerked and toppled to the parking lot. A hairy, overweight guy next to the van followed suit, 2-Patti's bullet taking him in the jaw.

While 31-Patti had to work the action on her 700, 2-Patti popped off four more shots and made four more kills. The Free Staters stared around in confusion, trying to simultaneously duck and see who was picking them off. 31-Patti took out another sheep from their fold.

"Shit!" screamed a scrawny young Free Stater. He couldn't have been more than twenty. He and three of his doubles scrambled into the panel van. One of them got the engine going while a dozen of his comrades outside yelled at him to stop, calling him a coward.

He wasn't a coward. He was smart. He squealed out of the lot, taking two-thirds of the Free Staters' cover with him.

2-Patti continued firing, squeezing off even bursts, syncing them with her breaths. Free Staters fell like pine cones, taking fire from two sides as the defenders in the store increased their volley.

Another three seconds and the truth finally dawned on the eleven men remaining in the parking lot. They were either going to run or die. Their chance for victory was gone.

One of them, a large white man dressed in camo coveralls, screamed something 2-Patti couldn't make out, and they headed for their trucks. A shot from inside the store dropped another one before they could follow the kid they had called a coward, leaving their dead behind. 31-Patti started to fire at their retreating vehicles, but 2-Patti waved her off.

Five men and three women exited the wrecked storefront. Four of the men were the same tall, lanky white guy with gray hair and dark blue eyes. Each carried a matching Winchester rifle.

"Patty Cake!" said three of the Colonel Andrew Boyds at once. All four jogged to meet 2 and 31-Patti in the lot.

The Pattis assumed a position of attention and rendered a military salute sharp enough to slice bread, which made the colonels laugh. They returned the salute.

"Haven't seen you in three months, Sergeant," one of the colonels said to 2-Patti while the others started talking with her harmony mates.

"Been busy with the wedding," 2-Patti said. She lifted an eyebrow. "Are you 1-Andrew by chance?"

He shook his head with a wry grin. "I'm 52. Sorry we couldn't make the wedding, by the way. As you can see, we've been busy." He waved a hand at the blood, bodies, and tire marks on the asphalt. "Thanks for the assist."

"Anytime," 2-Patti said, though she was feeling some regret at how much ammo that little action had cost her. 1-Patti would have found a way to end the firefight without such expense. "I had no idea the Free Staters had gasoline."

"They've got a stash of Pri-G. I don't think they have much, but they're willing to use it against us. They think my town belongs to them."

2-Patti could understand why. Anderson, South Carolina was one of the only peaceful cities she knew of. And it owed that peace to Colonel Boyd and his harmony. Patti had never served under the colonel in active service, he was a Marine, but she had come to respect his leadership since X-Day.

"So what brings you here?" 52-Andrew asked. "I get the feeling you didn't come to reminisce about old times."

"1-Patti's gone missing."

"Missing how?"

"You heard about that church down in Star-Iva? The one supposed to be growing all sorts of food?"

"Yeah. We've got some trade going with them. Can't say I like it much though."

"Why?" 2-Patti asked.

"I've been hearing things about them—talk of rekindling that Birth Rights nonsense from back at the beginning. You think 1-Patti joined them?"

2-Patti shook her head, keenly aware of her harmony listening to their conversation. "I don't know."

"So why did you come here?" 52-Andrew asked.

"Ain't that a good question," 23-Patti said to the empty air over one shoulder.

"I need to know the layout of the place. What sort of security they got there? How many harmonies? That sort of thing. I could use your help planning what to do."

52-Andrew eyed her for a long moment. Then he motioned for 2-Patti to follow him into the ruined store away from the others. When they were out of earshot, he rounded on her. "Is something wrong with you, soldier?"

"No, sir. I'm just—"

"Sergeant First Class Cook, did you really just ruck march to Anderson when your primary target is miles from here? You're special forces. Is there anything I could tell you about this church that you couldn't have found on your own?"

"Colonel, I—"

52-Andrew held up a hand. "Don't even start with whatever bullshit was about to pour out of your mouth. You think I don't recognize a crisis of confidence when I see one? You're not her, am I right?"

2-Patti's throat constricted the way it always did whenever a superior dressed her down. "No, sir. I'm not her. I'm me."

"Number two. Second best. Is that it?" 52-Andrew asked.

2-Patti shook her head, though a small voice inside whispered that it was true.

"Bull. You think it every minute you're awake. I'm number fifty-two in my harmony. I know how it feels. It's easy to start thinking you're not as good as your One—that you're not real. But you got to stomp that shit right out of your head now, Sergeant. You're about to lead your sisters into an unknown. You can't doubt yourself. You are Patti Cook. You've got everything she's got. You either believe that and make it true, or you wither away into a shell of yourself. Which is it?"

"She's better at—"

"Bullshit. Step up, Sergeant."

2-Patti swallowed. Her throat felt suddenly dry. "I will, sir."

"You'd better. Now, I can't do a lot to help you. My resources are strapped keeping this town safe. But I'll replace the ammo you spent saving us, and I think we can spare you a couple of radios. After that, you need to get the hell out of my town and get your ass on task." 52-Andrew said this without rancor. He even spared 2-Patti a slight grin when she looked up.

"I will, sir."

IV

Patti Harmony reached the outskirts of Starr, South Carolina at 0930 the next morning. Like most towns in the deep south after X-Day, Starr was rural, impoverished to the point of daily death tolls, and starving. Indolent harmonies gathered outside their makeshift homes in abandoned gas stations and storefronts to watch the Pattis. Many of the women had squalling infants in their arms or small kids chasing

69

about. 2-Patti shook her head at that. How anyone could bring a child into this world was beyond her.

They reached a widened stretch of asphalt where SC HWY 81 merged into Starr's main road, Stones Throw Avenue. 2-Patti lifted a fist to call a halt.

"Okay, we're going to split up," she said. "I want four of you with me—not you, 23, I'm sorry."

23-Patti put her hands on her hips. "Don't be leaving me out, 2."

"If this is leaving you out then I'm doing it to nearly everybody," 2-Patti said. "26, 45, 60, and 31 you're with me. The rest are in reserve. Make camp nearby and be listening for my signal. If things go south for us with this church, I'll radio."

"You sure about this?" 34-Patti asked. "Maybe we should all go—power in numbers and all."

"No. I'm not sure about any of this, but I know I'll want backup if things go pear-shaped. Better if ya'll are a surprise."

"I know, Mama, but she don't listen to me," 23-Patti said loud enough for everybody to hear.

2-Patti rolled her eyes. "Just say whatever you're gonna say, 23."

"It ain't me!" 23-Patti looked offended. "It's Mama-Gloria from my dimension."

"Fine. What does Mama-Gloria from the 23rd dimension have to say about my plan?"

"She say, 'Don't these church people already know about all of us since they got 1-Patti and the others?'"

"Maybe," 2-Patti said. "But we don't know what we don't know, right? That's the oldest problem for any army. Maybe our sisters told them about us, and maybe they didn't. Either way, I think we're better off going into the unknown with something in reserve."

23-Patti stared off into space for a moment, nodding. "Mama say, 'You the sergeant, and maybe you know more,' but she also say, 'You crazy for not taking 23 with you.' Now that wasn't me, that was Mama-Gloria."

2-Patti smiled and hugged 23. "I know you want to go to protect me, but you can do that better as backup. All right?"

23-Patti nodded.

The harmony split, and 2-Patti led her four sisters into the town proper, which was little more than a weedy wide spot in the road.

A crowd of children—there must have been fifty of them, dressed in rags and so caked with dirt and grime they looked like war refugees—abandoned their play in the street to follow.

"Who are you?" asked a little blonde girl.

"You a soldier?" asked a dark-haired boy wearing a Spider-Man pajama top two sizes too small.

Most of the children bore those two faces. They were likely brother and sister from the look of them. Their exponents were just as full of questions. It was like rolling into Baghdad when all the kids would come dancing out of alleyways begging for candy and patting you with their little hands.

"We don't have anything," 30-Patti and 31-Patti said at the same time.

"Is there a church around here? One that's been growing a lot of food?" 2-Patti asked.

"Oh, yeah, them cult people." The blonde girl gave 2-Patti a confiding smirk.

One of the boys shushed her. "We ain't supposed to talk about them, Rubyanne. Mama said so."

Several of the Rubyannes shrugged while others gave the boy a roll of their eyes. Their movements were so coordinated, it made 2-Patti smile. These kids probably couldn't remember much of the world without doubles. Communication like this was second nature to them.

"Mama does say they're a cult," confided the Rubyanne speaking with 2-Patti. "But they got food, so everybody trades with 'em."

"Where's their church?"

The nearest Rubyanne pointed along Stones Throw Ave. "Straight that way and then left at Smith McGee Road. You can't miss it. They got a big white wall and two huge buildings and lots of people out working in the fields all dressed like pilgrims."

"Thank you. Are you 1-Rubyanne?"

The little girl shrugged. "I dunno."

"We lost track," said one of her doubles.

29-Patti raised her eyebrows at that.

"I guess kids aren't so concerned about who's who," 2-Patti said. She refrained from adding, *Maybe adults could learn something from that.*

71

V

The church was indeed surrounded by a stone wall just as Rubyanne had promised. It was whitewashed and stood ten feet high. Rusty razor wire snaked along its top.

"We're not getting over that without trouble," 48-Patti said.

"And not without knowing what's on the other side," 2-Patti said.

Hundreds of men and women, many of them duplicates of one another, worked in a field opposite the wall, tilling the land with hoes and shovels. Rubyanne proved right again. These farmhands were dressed conservatively, but not like pilgrims, more like Amish or plain folk. The men wore black pants and vests with colored button-up shirts. Most had long beards and shaggy hair. The women wore long skirts of gray, blue, or black. And not one was bareheaded—they all wore bonnets that tied under their chins to cover their hair.

"You think they're slaves?" 26-Patti whispered to 2.

2-Patti shook her head. "Probably not. I don't see anybody watching them. If they're slaves, where're the overseers?"

"I think we might be about to find out," 34-Patti said.

A small crowd, maybe 150 to 200 people, had gathered in front of a swing arm gate set into the wall. They weren't dressed like the farmers, but wore the usual assortment of post-X fashions: worn blue jeans, tennis shoes that had seen too many miles, shirts streaked with stains, and hats to deflect the sun. They stank of sour sweat—a stench every Patti knew.

"This the revival meeting?" 45-Patti asked a black woman who looked to be in her sixties.

Three of her turned to smile and say, "Yeah, honey."

"You'll have to check your weapons," said a burly man dressed like the farmers across the street. He and one of his harmony mates strolled along the line with several others, pushing wheelbarrows full of guns, knives, chains, and even a few rocks.

All the Pattis looked to 2-Patti at this news.

"We get them back?" 2-Patti asked.

The man nodded. One of his doubles, who bore a deep scar down his left cheek that his twin didn't have, said, "Yes. We'll give you chit for it."

A military guy, then. That didn't mean 2-Patti could trust him, or any of his ilk, but it eased her mind. Slightly.

"Okay," 2-Patti said. She put on a brave face, and handed the scarred man her M4. He passed her back a handwritten note with its make and serial number printed in blocky letters. At 2-Patti's example, the other Pattis gave up their few guns and many knives.

A band started to play from somewhere behind the wall, picking out a twangy version of Amazing Grace with guitars and banjos.

"Oh, it's starting!" said one of the old women.

Someone opened the gate from the inside to reveal an acre of green grass that rolled up to a white, three story building. The place was ostentatious. It didn't belong in Starr, that was certain. It looked like someone had either copied an old world European cathedral, or moved an original one here brick-by-brick. Honest to God castle turrets stood at each of its four corners with crenelated tops and small stained glass windows set into their stones.

"Wow," 64-Patti said. "They're really going for awe factor here, aren't they?"

"I guess this is their temple," 2-Patti said.

Her harmony nodded their heads.

"Looks like they got power too," 31-Patti said, pointing to a row of windmills that dominated several acres of the walled-in property.

"You can't pump out good gospel music without an amp," 29-Patti said.

One of the old women doubles within earshot gave her a dirty look and 2-Patti signaled for her harmony to be silent. They didn't need any more complications than they already had.

A stage stood in front of the temple. It had all the trappings of a pre-X concert with it's multi-colored lights set into the roof, microphones on stands, and speakers as tall as Patti. A large, enclosed tent, nearly the size of a big top at a pre-X circus, stood next to the stage. Some in the crowd headed toward it, but were shooed away by a covey of conservatively dressed women.

"This way, folks," said one black woman dressed in a long blue skirt and head covering.

"Sorry, we don't have any chairs," said another of her.

"You won't miss them," said a third. "You'll be having too much fun!"

Patty Harmony stuck together, as did most of the harmonies in the crowd. They ended up relatively close to the stage, standing with the woman who had spoken to them outside.

"This your first time coming here?" asked one of the old woman's exponents.

2-Patti nodded.

"They got a good message and a good preacher. We just aren't sure we're ready for all he's asking of us."

"What do you mean—" 2-Patti started to ask, but was cut off when a tall, well-muscled white man took the stage and the crowd burst into enthusiastic applause.

He wore a fine suit. It was steel gray with a crease down each leg. His gold tie complimented his watch and rings. His shoes were polished, his teeth were white, and he looked like he had been eating well.

60-Patti leaned and whispered in 2-Patti's ear, "Now that's a preacher."

"How y'all doing?" he asked in a voice that was deep and rich.

The crowd again exploded in raucous cheers and applause.

He smiled and pulled the main microphone from its stand. "For y'all that don't know me, my name's Reverend Phillip Sligh."

The crowd tried to cheer again, but Sligh held up his hands. "Y'all come here for a revival meeting, but I'm here to tell you this ain't about revival, it's about survival, brothers and sisters."

A chorus of "Amen!" and "Preach it, brother!" rang from the crowd.

"Old ways are what got us into this mess. Old ways were sin and lasciviousness. I'm telling you all now, the exponents, as the great minds of our day call them, are not evil as some have preached. But they are a curse put upon this world by the everliving God—a curse that nevertheless brings with it a message of hope and gladness for the eternities.

"Now, some of you might already have heard the good news. Maybe some folks told you that the Church of the Sanctified One was a cult—that we're spreading lies and making slaves of people."

A few in the crowd—2-Patti noted with interest that they were dressed ultra-conservatively—laughed at this, or shouted, "Ain't true," or "Lies!"

"If devotion to the one everliving, everloving, everlasting God in heaven is a lie, then make me a slave today, brothers and sisters!" Sligh shouted the words, making them ring across the crowd. He turned then and waved his hand at the entrance to the tent.

A line of Reverend Phillip Sligh's exponents marched onto the stage. Each wore the same plaid shirt with plain black pants and work boots. They walked quickly, forming up behind their double with the microphone, but it still took nearly a minute for them to all assemble. The crowd began to murmur and makes sounds of surprise as the seconds passed and the trickle of Slighs continued. The last to appear brought his well-dressed double on the stage a bottle of water.

"Thank you, 64," Sligh said.

"Did you count them?" 45-Patti whispered. "There's 64 of them."

2-Patti had counted, but was doubting her tally. "That's not possible. Nobody has a perfect 64." Colonel Boyd had the most complete harmony she had ever seen, and his harmony boasted only about fifty exponents.

Sligh let the moment last a little longer, taking a slow sip of water. He put the bottle down next to his mic stand, and when he turned back to the crowd, he had assumed a grave expression. "You see, brothers and sisters, I am a blessed man. God has sheltered my harmony with His own hand from the breaking of mankind so that we can bring you His new message—His new dispensation. Forget what you've been told about me and our church. Let God himself explain the hurt and heartache and sacrifice you've been living through lo these last four years."

"You've all heard about the war in heaven. You know that the souls who fought against our Father God were sent to the fiery pit with their foul master, Satan. And that the good souls who remained valiant sons and daughters were allowed to come down to this Earth to be tried. Those are the Ones, brothers and sisters. Some of you are Ones. Most of you are not. Now, don't despair, thinking I've tricked you somehow—that I'm against exponents. Brothers and sisters, some of my dearest friends are exponents!"

Sligh's army of doubles laughed on cue, and 2-Patti felt her stomach go tight. No matter what he said, she was certain it wasn't going to be equality for exponents, not with him standing there in his thousand dollar suit and Rolex watch.

"There has been a second war in heaven, y'all," Sligh said. "A second war in which the forces of the evil one connived and wrangled many good souls to rail against our Father which art in heaven. Now I don't know the minds of demons. I can't think how they imagined they would overthrow the architect of the universe, and they didn't. God's forces bested them four years ago. The evil souls who came against our Father were banished back to hell fire. But those souls who had served God valiantly in the first war, only to turn traitor during this second conflict, begged for mercy. God, being ever beneficent, decided to make an example of these souls, both to the living and the dead. He sent them here not as individuals, for they did not deserve such in his estimation. Instead, they became copies of those who had gone before."

Another round of murmuring broke out in the crowd, this time much less pleased sounding than before.

"I knew it," 2-Patti said.

"I know some of you Ones, your exponents won't hear of serving. They say they're people just like you, and to that I say, it's true. It's true they are people, they deserve dignity. But what of their souls, brothers and sisters? They fought against the Most High and lost. They were sent here as copies of copies as punishment for that sin! To serve is to live everlasting life. You exponents who have taken your rightful place, I bless you in the name of Jesus, for you have chosen the hard path— the hard way! And you will be returned to your Father in heaven triumph amongst the brothers or sisters of your harmony, a peer and an equal in the kingdom come."

"You buying this crap, 2?" 64-Patti asked.

"Hello no," 2-Patti said. She had to purposefully stop grinding her teeth as the preacher continued. "I've heard enough. Let's see if we can scout around a little. Maybe one of us will spot 1-Patti."

"Uh, 2," 48-Patti said, pointing a shaking finger at the stage.

Apparently, Sligh had called for testimonies from members of his ridiculous church while 2-Patti wasn't listening. 1-Patti, dressed like an Amish woman, exited the tent with a radiant smile creasing her dark cheeks. She strode to Sligh's side with purpose, and he handed her the microphone.

"Hello, my name's Patti Cook." She focused her gaze on her harmony mates. "Pattis. I knew you'd come. Welcome home."

A commotion in the crowd caught 2-Patti's attention. Dozens of church members in their plain attire were converging on Patti Harmony. A large black man caught 45-Patti by the arm. She tried to resist, but three of his doubles got hands on her.

Some in the crowd protested, but none offered help. They spread out in a circle to watch the spectacle.

"Patti!" shouted 2-Patti. "Why are you doing this? What have they done?"

"Don't resist them," 1-Patti said into the microphone. "No one's going to hurt you. We just need to talk."

An average-sized white guy and two of his doubles surrounded 2-Patti. She didn't give them time to formulate a plan. She kicked the one in front of her in the knee and spun him bodily into the others. Then she keyed the radio at her throat. "The Jaybird sings!"

Static crackled in her ear as she dodged the grasp of a small woman, only to have a set of triplets, each the size of a small boulder, lift her bodily from the ground. The men were too strong for her to mount any sort of effective defense. It was like she was a two-year-old resisting a parent.

Desperately, she keyed the radio a second time. "Pattis! The Jaybird sings!"

The sound of 2-Patti's voice, tinny and static filled, erupted from somewhere nearby. Even as she struggled in vain to resist the triplets, 2-Patti searched the crowd until her gaze found her own eyes staring back.

At least fifty cultists stood in a semi-circle off to one side of the stage, pointing an assortment of rifles and handguns at the exponents 2-Patti had left in the woods. Nearly all of Patti Harmony was there except for one or two—it was hard to tell even for her. 23-Patti must have run off. She was probably scared out of her mind, what was left of it right now. Poor thing.

"Stop fighting," 2-Patti said to the rest of her sisters. They too had seen the hostages. Most had already quit, but at 2-Patti's order, the rest fell still.

"This is for the best, Patti," 1-Patti said from the stage. "We're going to be happy. You'll see."

VI

"Why are you doing this?" 2-Patti struggled against the three burly men hustling her toward the temple. She could just see 1-Patti behind her, strolling with 1-Phillip at her side.

"That's my 2," 1-Patti said to 1-Phillip.

1-Phillip pointed at the temple doors. His men separated Patti Harmony, 2-Patti's abductors hauling her inside while scores of other cultists dragged the other Pattis toward a long row of trailers—a real eyesore—behind the temple.

The temple smelled like sawdust and new paint. Electric lights burned overhead, throwing an unnatural glow over gilded portraits of Jesus and saints and depictions of bible stories hanging in the vestibule. The men carried 2-Patti up a flight of stairs that opened into a hallway on the second floor. Their footfalls echoed in the dim corridor.

They passed several doorways with small, shatterproof windows set at eye level. 2-Patti thought she glimpsed one of her harmony mates through one of the windows, but couldn't be certain. They had moved on before she got a good look.

The men shoved Patti into a cell five doors down and on the right. They forced her into a chair that looked like it belonged in a dentist's office. One of the doubles held her still while two of them secured 2-Patti's wrists and ankles with leather straps.

2-Patti kept calm. She wanted answers. She wasn't going to get them if she fought.

1-Patti eyed her, no doubt surmising her exponent's thoughts without effort.

Two white women dressed in floral-patterned scrubs entered the room. One carried what 2-Patti at first took for a small pistol in one hand. But no, it was some sort of medical device. It was brown and white, with a hand grip on one end and a flared tip. A light glowed green on one side of the thing.

The second woman, twin to the first, pulled a syringe and several empty vials from a scrubs pocket.

2-Patti's heart sped up. She swallowed.

"Shall I, Phillip?" asked the twin with the gun.

1-Phillip nodded gravely.

The nurse rolled 2-Patti's sleeve up to expose her biceps.

"What is this?" 2-Patti asked 1-Patti. She could no longer fight the feelings of betrayal pervading her emotions.

"It's a test," 1-Phillip said, "to determine the probability that you are the One from your harmony.

"You think 1-Patti lied to you?"

"We can never be too sure," 1-Phillip said. "A lot of exponents would like to be the One. And sometimes, with all the confusion in this fallen world, people forget their rightful number. It's understandable. You share your original's memories, after all."

The nurse pressed the gun's tip against 2-Patti's exposed skin and pulled the trigger. There followed a static burp, a sting of pain, and the odor of burnt flesh.

2-Patti clenched her teeth.

"Sorry," the nurse said. "It cauterizes after taking the sample. Don't worry, though, it won't leave a scar."

"I thought there was no way to tell us apart," 2-Patti said, still looking at 1-Patti.

1-Phillip grinned, probably at the way 2-Patti refused to look at him. "A handful of firms scrambled to solve the problem right before the great collapse. That one is called a Divisor. It's a prototype created by Clarke Glaxor and Kline, the pharmaceutical lab. It's quite reliable. I've tested it against my own harmony several times."

The second nurse tied a thick rubber band about 2-Patti's upper arm and proceeded to search for a vein.

"If it works so well, why do you need to draw blood?"

"The Divisor isn't perfect. We have a second means of determining your place with a blood sample, but it takes a few days to complete."

The second nurse swabbed 2-Patti's inner elbow with a musty smelling suave then pushed the needled into her vein. Blood bubbled up into its vial, driven hard by her speeding heart.

"This is all lies," 2-Patti said to her original. "You know I'm not an exponents rights nut, but we're people just like you. We're equal."

"I know you are," 1-Patti said, the sincerity on her face and in her voice genuine and sad. "And you will be equal in the eternities."

The nurse switched out vials on the syringe, sending a stinging tingle of pain up 2-Patti's arm.

"But just not here and now?" 2-Patti said, grimacing.

"Exponents must pay a price in servitude for their actions in the second heavenly war," 1-Phillip said, his eyes suddenly full of fervor.

"Bullshit," 2-Patti said. "Who the hell are you, anyway? You made this shit up and now you've got your own harmony believing it, and all these gullible people. It's insane."

"It's the gospel," 1-Patti said, slowly shaking her head with pity.

The machine in the first nurse's hands beeped. She peered at a small screen on its back end for a second, then smiled. "This is almost definitely one of Patti's exponents. Probability is in the high nineties."

"How does it tell that?" 2-Patti asked.

"The Divisor measures the telomeres in your DNA," said one nurse.

"They're little end caps on the strands," said the other.

"The older you are, the shorter your telomere caps. Exponents have abnormally long ones. Makes it easy to tell them apart from originals," said the first.

"Good," 1-Phillip said with a smile. "Then we know we're dealing with 2-Patti after all."

A look of relief passed over 1-Patti's features.

"You were worried we had gotten mixed up somewhere along the way," 2-Patti said. "Afraid you might be the one made a slave?"

1-Phillip shook his head, his lips turned down in mild reproof. "No one on church premises is a slave, Patti. The exponents here serve willingly, because they share faith in the gospel. "I know you find that hard to understand right now. But I think you'll come around. Your One has."

"My *One* has lost her mind. And what you're doing here is wrong."

"You witnessed my harmony," 1-Phillip said. "We are a perfect 64."

"So?"

"How can you believe that possible outside of divine intervention? We made it through the plagues, wars, and civil unrest of the last four years unscathed. Have you ever heard of another harmony to have done that? God protected us for His grand purpose."

"You hid somewhere like a bunch of cowards. Probably refused to help anyone but yourselves the whole time."

1-Phillip shook his head slowly, a beautific smile on his face—the indulgent father suffering his daughter's tirade with good humor and patience. He stepped forward to gently place his hand on 2-Patti's cheek. "I know you, Patti, because I know your One. She is tough as old hickory, and dangerous in ways I and my harmony can't even imagine. But she's also kind and contemplative—the sort who will put herself in danger to protect a co-op of farmers whom she could have ruled had she but wished it. She, and her harmony, are just what the Church of the Anointed One need right now—just what I need right now. 1-Patti will be my general. She will run my armies, command the Church's foot soldiers. And you will be her adjunct. Together, we will feed and protect the masses. Isn't that exactly what you're trying to do already? Join with us, and we will reunite the world under our banner."

2-Patti gritted her teeth through Phillip's sermon. Rage boiled inside her. This man was a charlatan. How could 1-Patti not see that? Was she so enamored with the idea of command that the possibility was blinding her? Maybe they really were different after all. 2-Patti couldn't imagine ever joining this man. He would never have her loyalty.

Giving him no warning, 2-Patti jerked her head to the side and bit into 1-Phillip's thumb. She didn't stint, but ground her teeth, jerking her head side-to-side. She tasted blood.

1-Phillip screamed. He struggled to free his hand while his stunned guards looked on in horror, seemingly too shocked to react for a several seconds.

Then a hard fist connected with the side of 2-Patti's head. She lost consciousness for maybe half a second, blotches of swirling black and purple threatening to swallow her vision. When she came to, 1-Phillip stood cradling his bloodied hand against his expensive suit coat, while 1-Patti held 2-Patti's head back by the hair, fist raised to deliver another blow.

"Goddamn that bitch!" 1-Phillip roared.

"You don't touch him," 1-Patti said, wrenching 2-Patti's hair with each syllable. "You don't deserve to touch him!"

Despite the physical pain, despite the feeling of utter betrayal that made her want to curl into a ball and wither away like a grape, and despite the fear she was too proud to admit was turning her insides into jelly, 2-Patti smiled. She could taste blood on her teeth—Phillip's blood—and she hoped it showed. "Go to hell, sister."

VII

They did a good job of chaining her up. Padded leather cuffs kept 2-Patti's arms above her head with just enough slack so that she could either stand or hang, but never sit. A matching set of manacles bound her ankles. They kept her in place, unable to do more than shift her weight from one painfully aching leg to the other.

Was 1-Patti behind the arrangement? Maybe. 1-Phillip, or perhaps some of his flunkies, might have designed it, but this sort of enhanced interrogation device had devious Ranger written all over it.

2-Patti would have thought of it.

She heaved a sigh, rolling her shoulders to coax some blood flow. Her hands had gone from pins and needles to severe pain hours ago with only a brief, and again painful, reprieve. Now they were lifeless things, numb as two dead fish hanging on hooks.

She couldn't tell the time, which was frustrating. The room had no windows nor clocks. The walls were smooth and white. 1-Phillip had even ordered his guards to remove the chair where the nurse had drawn 2-Patti's blood, making the most interesting thing in the place its bland carpet decorated in squares of varying shades of tan.

The room was silent except for the rasp of 2-Patti's breathing and the chain rattling when she moved. It had been a long time since she had experienced silence. That was a rare commodity in a world so filled with people.

2-Patti hated it.

She could hear her heart beating, and the hollow gurgling in her stomach. She hadn't eaten since before she arrived at the compound. That too was part of the torture. No sleep, no food, no dignity.

The cultists had allowed her to use the toilet once. Six women, all from the same harmony, had stripped her clothes away and hustled her down the hall, naked save for the chains, to a small lavatory. They had watched her do her business then hustled her back. Her door guards, the three burly guys who had carried her here, had gotten an eyeful. The women had drawn a near see-through shift over 2-Patti's head before chaining her back to the wall.

The worst part was understanding what was happening and remaining powerless to change it. Beyond the discomfort, the pain, the psychological aspects, there laid the mindfulness. 2-Patti could know what was happening to her—she had seen it happen to detainees back in Afghanistan—but that knowledge hardly made a difference. Her body reacted like any other body in this situation, and that included her brain. She was strong now, but eventually she would break—was already breaking.

2-Patti let her body hang from the wrist straps for a few seconds, knees bent, toes on the floor, giving her hips and back a short-lived reprieve from holding her up. Her shoulders screamed in pain. Her arms and hands felt nothing, which was probably worse. A cramp flared in her hip. She got her feet back on the floor, but could do nothing to work out the clenching muscle. She groaned.

As if in answer, 2-Patti heard a sound outside her door. Several sounds, really. First came a thump, followed by the echo of scuttling feet, a deep-throated cry of alarm or anger, then several more thumps.

2-Patti's cell door swung open and 23-Patti sauntered inside wearing a long ocher robe that could have been a dress except it was split down the middle to reveal her regular clothes beneath. She carried a length of wood in one hand and a Colt .45 in the other.

"Rangers, lead the way," 23-Patti said, her mismatched eyes sparkling. She flourished her stick, which 2-Patti suddenly realized was a policeman's club, once around her wrist like a cheerleader's baton then shoved it into the belt of her camo booty shorts. "Hi, sis. Miss me?"

2-Patti couldn't smile. She was in too much pain. But she shook with relief at seeing her harmony mate.

5-Patti entered the door behind 23. She gasped when she saw 2-Patti and hurried over with a set of keys she must have pilfered from the guards outside.

2-Patti groaned when they helped her drop her arms. They eased her to the floor, 5-Patti bracing her so that she wouldn't crack her head open.

23-Patti stood next to the cell door, humming to herself, alternately peeking out and stealing glances at 2-Patti.

"I'm sorry we didn't get here faster," 5-Patti whispered. She fished a squeeze bottle from the pack she wore and gave 2-Patti a sip.

"How?" 2-Patti croaked. She hadn't realized just how dry and sore her throat felt.

"23," 5-Patti said, nodding at their harmony mate. "She hauled me off into the woods when those cultists came to round us up. We kept hidden until it was clear. We stole some clothes from a line and walked in the front gate dressed all Polly Pilgrim. Nobody said a thing to us."

"Believe me, nobody questions dirt," 23-Patti said. "We look like nothing, then we ain't worth talking to."

"And you just walked in here?" 2-Patti asked.

5-Patti shook her head. "It wasn't that easy. We had to do some sneaking to get in this place, but these people have shoddy security."

"They wasn't nobody guarding the rooms downstairs," 23-Patti said. "They had three guards on this hall, but didn't none of them know how to fight. They all laying out in the hallway right now. If one moves, I'll bop him."

"Where are 1-Patti and the others?" 5-Patti asked. She gave 2-Patti another drink.

"1-Patti's aligned herself with these freaks," 2-Patti said. "I think some of the others are locked in cells on this floor."

"1-Patti's part of this?"

Some feeling was coming back into 2-Patti's arms and hands. They hurt like hell, and she had no fine motor skills whatsoever, but she could move them a bit. That was a start. "Yes, but we'll talk about it later. Help me up."

2-Patti couldn't make a fist, and she required 5-Patti's help just to walk, but together the three of them exited the room.

23-Patti leveled her Colt on the nearest guard who was starting to rouse. "Shoot him?"

2-Patti shook her head. "No. We're not murdering anybody."

23-Patti frowned. She looked put out.

"The sound will draw attention," 2-Patti said.

"Oh. That's true," 23-Patti said. She squatted in front of the big man who had just opened his eyes. "You move and I'll beat you to death with my nightstick. That won't make enough noise to be heard outside."

The man, who had obviously already seen the nasty end of 23-Patti's club as evidenced by several cuts and nascent purple bruises on his face, nodded and remained still.

5-Patti began opening cell doors. It was slow going. The things had old-fashioned key locks, forcing her to try key after key until she struck pay dirt.

None of the other Pattis had been tortured like 2-Patti. The cultists had dressed them in shifts, given them little food and water, and no creature comforts, not even cots to sleep on, but none wore chains. So that was to the good.

The reunion was truncated. 2-Patti allowed for, and shared in, a few hugs and even some tears, but the harmony wasn't safe here. Every sound they made put her nerves on edge.

She took a quick head count to busy her mind. They were ten mostly unarmed, hungry, and hurting women. They faced an unknown number of enemy zealots, at least one of whom was the OG Patti Cook, and they were miles from home.

"That's enough, ladies," she said. The harmony grew still, and 2-Patti felt suddenly uncomfortable under their scrutiny. What would 1-Patti do in this situation. Would she—

2-Patti squashed the thought. She refused to fall back on her old ways of thinking. What would 1-Patti do? She would turn against her own harmony to follow some whack job of a cult leader who thought the bulk of humans alive today should be slaves.

Screw that.

"Okay. Here's what we're going to do."

VIII

The temple was empty and only lightly guarded on the outside. 2-Patti outlined a search plan, splitting her harmony by twos. They found what she wanted on the first floor in a set of offices built behind the temple's vainglorious east wall. One of the rooms was filled to the gilded ceiling with medical supplies, including a crash cart, hundreds of syringes and small boxes of medicines with names the Pattis couldn't pronounce, and other med tech.

"They must have raided a hospital early on," 64-Patti said.

"Or a pharmacy," 33-Patti said.

2-Patti ignored them. Her mind was reeling with possibilities. Part of her wanted to strip this place clean. They had no doctors back on the co-op, but Cecelia Flint had been a Physician's Assistant for twenty years leading up to X-Day. Her harmony would know what to do with this stuff. But stealing it meant taking it away from all the people living here. Just because they were following a cult leader didn't mean they deserved to be harmed.

"You thinking we should take it?" 27-Patti asked.

The question almost cracked 2-Patti's resolve. She nearly gave her harmony mates the go-ahead to take all they could carry. It would be that easy. One domino tumbles and the whole line goes down.

She drew a deep breath, and shook her head. "No. We've got no reason to harm these people."

"How about them holding us prisoner?" 13-Patti asked.

"And torturing you," 18-Patti said.

2-Patti slipped a small, brown satchel from a peg on the wall. The DNA testing gun, 1-Phillip had called it the Divisor, lay snug inside. It was a near priceless object in this ruined world.

She slipped the satchel over one shoulder. "No. We're taking what we came for and getting back to the co-op."

"Now all we need is a Phillip," 23-Patti said, her lips curled at the edges in a malicious little grin.

2-Patti grinned right back. "Let's go find one."

IX

The temple guards were big and armed, but stupid and blind. Patti Harmony took out all five inside two minutes. They were all from one harmony, a musclebound Chicano with a jagged scar under his right eye. He must have thought it made him look tough, but it didn't do a thing for his abilities. The Pattis tied the five together using their own flannel shirts and locked them in a temple cell. They managed it without a shot fired.

"Now what?" 5-Patti asked. She stood at the temple entrance, a Kalashnikov resting on one shoulder.

"Take everyone but 23—check out those trailers behind this building," 2-Patti said. "I have a feeling the rest of our harmony's there, and probably a lot more to boot. If the patrols here are any indication, you shouldn't have any trouble. Bring any who can fight. If there are any casualties, we'll deal with them later."

The others wanted to protest, but 2-Patti cut them off.

"We need numbers if we're going to win free of this place. You've got your orders," she said, grinning to show it was a half a joke. "Lead the way."

X

The revival was once again in full swing. Amplified organ music reverberated around the compound. 2-Patti reconnoitered the stage from the leeward side of the temple, crouching in its shadow. 23-Patti squatted next to her, humming to herself and periodically whispering to someone who wasn't there.

Phillip's Harmony had already made their entrance. They stood behind the preacher in eight uniform rows on the stage while he harangued an audience of hundreds. Dozens of armed guards stood in front of the stage with others patrolling the outskirts.

"Here they come," 23-Patti whispered.

Their harmony came around the opposite side of the temple, 5-Patti in the lead. Her face was grim, but her eyes were bright.

"Is that everyone?" 2-Patti asked. Dozens of her were still streaming into view accompanied by exponents from a dozen other harmonies. They all looked starved and tired, their hair disheveled, their skin mottled with bruises. Each wore a thin shift, even the men.

"All of ours," 5-Patti said. "Some of the others were dead."

2-Patti cursed. "You explained the plan to them? Not everyone has to go. They can stay here if they want, or maybe head out if they think it's safe."

"I explained it. They're all in."

"Okay," 2-Patti said, nodding. "Let's do this."

XI

No one was more surprised than 23-Patti when 2-Patti handed her the Kalashnikov rifle. Her brown eyes went round as tennis balls.

"Stay near me," 2-Patti said. "I won't be able to handle a weapon for what I'm about to do."

"Yes, Sergeant," 23-Patti said, grinning. She cut her mismatched eyes to one side, looking off at nothing. "She trust me. I know. I know. Maybe she just desperate and needing backup, but she didn't ask 5-Patti, did she? She ask me—23!"

It felt good having her harmony around her. 2-Patti motioned for them to spread out on either flank. They did so with aplomb, shepherding the other exponents they had rescued to follow.

1-Phillip, who had been exhorting his parishioners to worship their Ones for the security of their everlasting souls, sputtered to a stop. "Guards! We have a situation!"

The crowd turned to face 2-Patti. She would not quell before them or before Phillip's bumbling guards who were trying, and mostly failing, to work their way through the people.

2-Patti pulled the Divisor from its case and held it aloft. It was clear the guards recognized it. Most of them stopped moving immediately. The crowd parted before her, egged on by armed versions of herself pushing them back, if not gently than with less force than they could have employed. She and 23-Patti approached the stage.

"You give that to my guards," 1-Phillip said. "You don't deserve to touch it, exponent."

"If one of your people even comes near me, this thing's going in the air. How many shots you think it will take my harmony to pulverize it?" 2-Patti asked.

1-Patti appeared from the nearby tent to climb the stage steps. She stood next to 1-Phillip, her eyes round with anger. "What the hell are you doing?"

2-Patti hesitated. She had always deferred to her original. The sight of 1-Patti's shock and anger gave her pause. But no. What was going on here wasn't right. And no matter how much it hurt to face the truth, 1-Patti was part of it all.

"What are we doing?" 2-Patti said, finding strength as she spoke. "The right thing!" She turned slowly, facing the crowd. "This man and his people tortured me and my harmony, and many other harmonies, all because we're exponents who refuse to worship our One. This device I'm holding can tell the difference between Ones and exponents. He's using it to divide harmonies and create slaves!"

Some in the crowd started to murmur. A couple of the guards and devout cultists raised voices of descent, but the Pattis shouted them down.

1-Philip drowned them all out with his amplified voice. "Lies. This woman was never tortured. No one was. I have simply tried my best, put forth my sincerest hand of friendship and guidance, to show her the way God would have her go." He lifted his hand over his head as if testifying in court.

23-Patti leaned closer to 2-Patti. "My Mama-Gloria say, 'Check out that preacher's hand—ain't no bite mark there.' She say the one you bit standing three Phillips from the right. You see that?"

2-Patti felt her eyes go round. 23-Patti was right. The Phillip holding the mike had unblemished hands. He wasn't 1-Phillip, or maybe he was. Either way, the one she had bitten stood just where 23-Patti said.

"They're taking turns," 2-Patti said.

23-Patti nodded. "King for a day."

"You're not a One!" 2-Patti shouted at Phillip.

The Phillip with the mike kept his composure, but his gaze flitted momentarily to the man 2-Patti had bitten. That one put his hands behind his back.

2-Patti turned to the crowd. "These men are lying to you! The one in front, he's not 1-Phillip. They're taking turns leading this cult."

The crowd looked about, gazing from 2-Patti to the Phillips and back. Even a few of Phillip's guards looked unsure.

"Get that woman out of here," shouted the Phillip with the mike. "She is disrupting a solemn meeting of God's chosen!"

"If you're a One, then you won't mind taking your own test," 2-Patti shouted, holding up the Divisor.

"I've no need to take it, Jezebel. I've proven myself to my disciples a hundred ways. Guards, get her out of here."

"I think he should take the test," shouted a man near the stage. He and four of his exponents sidled closer to 2-Patti, ignoring a female guard who trained her 12-guage rifle on him.

"Take the test!" 2-Patti shouted.

Others in the crowd echoed her, even a handful of the guards.

On stage, 1-Patti was staring at the Phillip holding the mike. Her mouth hung slightly open and she was standing rigid, the way she might if someone was threatening her.

He in turn looked pale, though two splotches of red tinged the points of his cheeks. He regarded the Phillip with the injured hand, his eyes pleading.

"That's 1-Phillip!" 2-Patti shouted, pointing the Divisor at him. She wasn't technically certain this was true, but it seemed likely, and from the way all the Phillips reacted, the look of surprise leapfrogging from one pallid face to the next, it had to be right.

"He ain't no prophet!" shouted 23-Patti.

"Take the test!" screamed a woman from somewhere in the back. Hers was the voice that sparked the chant. The crowd took it up as they pressed toward the stage. Most of the guards joined them. The few who tried to resist were ignored. Luckily, none were so enamored with Phillip that they were willing to kill in his defense.

Eight copies of the nurse who had tested 2-Patti with the Divisor melted out of the crowd. They were escorted by dozens of other cult members, their expressions ranging from angry to shocked to sorrowful.

"Can I have the gun?" asked one of the nurses, holding out her hand for the Divisor.

"We're going to test every one of them," said another.

2-Patti glanced at 23-Patti who shrugged then nodded. "I trust 'em. They look pissed."

2-Patti handed her the Divisor and the crowd split to let the nurses approach the stage. The test took no time. Three of the goon guards held the Phillip who had been on the mike in place while one of the nurses stuck him with the holy device.

"He's an exponent!" shouted the nurse.

A lot of shouting and roughhousing followed but, to 2-Patti's surprise, no gunfire. She signaled her harmony to draw back. They weren't part of this, not anymore.

1-Patti hopped down from the stage to approach them. Her face was ashy, her dark eyes forlorn.

"No," 30-Patti said, shaking her chin, "you don't come over here."

"You're not one of us, birther," 64-Patti said. "Take your sorry ass off with the rest of your kind. Uppity ones don't belong here."

2-Patti held up a hand and her harmony sisters quieted. She watched 1-Patti's eyes, her eyes, and waited.

"I believed him." 1-Patti's voice, usually so full of vigor, so forceful and commanding, warbled in her throat. "God forgive me, I did."

"No." By force of will, 2-Patti kept her tone even despite her roiling anger and hurt. "It was more than that. You wanted to believe him."

1-Patti looked at first shocked but then nodded. "Yes."

"You wanted to feel special."

"You're not." 30-Patti planted her hands on her hips, her jaw set.

1-Patti dropped her gaze. She didn't cry. She wouldn't. But her shoulders shook.

"Yes she is." 2-Patti's words drew shocked stares from the others. She ignored them. "She's Patti Cook."

"Hell no." 64-Patti rounded on 2-Patti. "I'm Patti Cook, and I wouldn't have acted like that. Neither would you. She lost all right to our name the second she betrayed our harmony."

"You're right."

"Huh?" 64-Patti looked surprised at the instant agreement. "Then we're kicking her out? No more co-op? No more harmony?"

A handful of the others nodded.

2-Patti shook her head. "No. I mean you're right when you say you're Patti Cook. Maybe you and I wouldn't have made the same choice as 1-Patti. But then again, maybe we would. What would any of us give to feel special? You all know what it's like living as an exponent. Just a copy of a copy of a copy. You think you wouldn't follow someone who told you different? Let me answer that. You don't know, because you've never been given the chance. We all think 16-Kenny's a dickhead—"

"I know that's right," 23-Patti said.

"—but he dotes on 8-Patti and she loves him for it."

The others shared meaningful looks. 2-Patti could see she had reached them—most of them anyway. 64-Patti wore a mulish expression 2-Patti had seen in the mirror far too often, but she would come around. Probably.

2-Patti turned her attention back to her wayward original. "You screwed up, Sergeant."

1-Patti nodded. She had to swallow a couple of times before she could speak. "I'm sorry. It's just this world, this terrible world—I don't feel like me anymore. I don't recognize that person."

"That's because there's only an us now." 2-Patti drew 1-Patti into her arms and held her.

"You'll take me back?"

"There'll be a price to pay. You'll have to make amends—show you're willing to work together. Things can't be like they were."

1-Patti drew back, her eyes gone wide. "But I can come home?"

2-Patti gripped 1-Patti's shoulders. "You are home, soldier."

"Oh, girl, move over." 23-Patti slipped between them to embrace 1-Patti. "You stupid, you know that?"

"Yeah, I know that." 1-Patti hugged 23 tight.

"My Mama Gloria say sometimes people got to learn a hard lesson to make a change, and sometimes it's other people what force that lesson on 'em." 23-Patti turned to 2-Patti, a knowing look in her healthy eye. "She say 1-Patti been acting stupid so you'd stop doing the same. And that worked out alright."

2-Patti smiled as the rest of her harmony mates, some with reluctance, others with enthusiasm, welcomed 1-Patti back into their fold. She nodded at 23. "Yeah, it did."

Room C
Daniel Arthur Smith

THERE WAS A TIME when I could navigate the endless twisting corridors of the Meg's massive ziggurats without losing my bearings, when the neural lace inlaid in my brain would propel me confidently into one pseudo-instinctual direction or another. But years of reliance on the nanos in my bloodstream have dulled my sense of direction as well as the memories of where I've been. Now that I'm older, I have to rely on the indicators on my ocular augments to show me when to turn. A HUD for the numb. So it was that when I reached the waiting room I had no sense of where I physically was, apart from the coordinates hovering in the corner of my eye. Without that mote, I'd have no north or south or altitude; the only tangible clue that I was in the Upper at all was the bland field of grey beyond the beaded outer glass.

The room was familiar, matching the broken images of a strained memory: the grey of the day falling pale over a dozen off-white plastic seats that lined the windowed wall; a door on the left—to the lavatory, the receptionist on the right, and behind her desk, the door to Room C.

There were two others already waiting, one in a vest and button down, the other, a bald man, in a white jumpsuit. Both were young looking; then again, with the age mods, we all look young. Both were occupying themselves with media. The first was swiping left across a screen implanted in his inner wrist. The other, the bald man, flipped channels by flicking his fingers in front of his face, paging through images hidden behind his milky blue eyes.

Neither acknowledged me, nor did the receptionist, her attention focused on the blue holo-console projected above her desktop.

Rather than assume an order, I ventured toward one of the open seats nearer the lavatory.

As I was about to sit, the receptionist cleared her throat. "Ahem," she said. She held a clear piece of digital glass in my direction which, when I approached, revealed itself to be a translucent questionnaire. Without making eye contact, she said, "Please answer all of the items."

"I'm in the system," I said, gesturing to her hovering console. "Number three. Zero-zero-three."

Her arm didn't waiver. "It's to verify," she said.

"But it doesn't seem—" THUMP!

The loud bump from the room behind her drew my attention to the door and the small lettered plaque affixed to it. A queasiness filled me. Rather than continue my protest I decided to take the glass pad and return to the seat I'd chosen when I walked in.

The questionnaire was not of the typical data gathering variety, querying my address and affiliation. Rather it was of the multiple choice type I'd taken there before—questions of taste concerning my favorite color or food or piece of clothing last year, last week, and now. Others asked how I felt about rabbits, children, dogs and turtles while others were ethical in nature. If I came across the same turtle on its back, what would I do? Some were seemingly nonsensical, such as which were smarter, dogs or cats—or turtles? The questions went on endlessly and seldom offered the exact answer I would have preferred, but they were calming and allowed me to pass the time in a Zen like state, checking off one box or another, then onto the next. So calm was I that when the sudden shriek came from the door beyond the receptionist, I jolted upright. My seatmates and I all looked to the door then to the receptionist who appeared unfazed. There was a second howl, followed by a series of low moans.

An excruciating buzz erupted from the same direction. The muscles in in my neck tightened and spasmed, and with a click, the door behind the receptionist swung ajar to reveal a tall thin man wearing black sunglasses and a shiny blue suit.

My augments kicked in, as they often do when someone abruptly enters, and as he crossed the room toward the lavatory, an overlay of a dozen or so translucent circles and squares covered the man.

My ocular implant assessed and, when the man closed the door behind him, discarded the data with no flags.

The bald man was the first to return to his viewer. He straightened his back, then again raised his hand to the field in front of his face and began to flick away what was only visible to him. Then the other man, the one in the vest seated closest to me, went back to the screen in his wrist. It occurred to me only then that they must have uploaded the same endless questionnaire the receptionist had given me.

The moans had faded, so I too put my attention back to my digital glass. But I had only just begun to read the next question—a choice between kittens and tigers—when the door to hallway opened and two hulking men, clad in surgical masks and loose-fitting white scrubs, entered with a gurney. Another deafening buzz pierced through me, and they entered Room C, leaving the door open. A shuffle and indiscernible muffled words followed, then they wheeled the gurney out—occupied and covered with a pink sheet. From beneath it came faint whimpers of, my guess, the man whose screams had filled the waiting room a moment before. The receptionist paid no mind as the huge men pushed the body cart past her and out into the hall.

The jet engine roar of a powerful blower erupted from within the lavatory. The blower ceased, the latch clicked, and the door slid open to reveal the blue suited man framed in tangerine light that blinked off when he exited the room.

He stepped toward the windowed wall, rubbing what I guessed to be disinfectant into his freshly dried hands. He stopped and fixed his gaze out to the grey beyond. Then without even so much as a nod, he marched past the three of us waiting in the row, beyond the receptionist, and without missing a stride, through the opened door behind her.

"Three," the receptionist said blandly. My attention shifted from the door to her. She hadn't lifted her head from her blue holo-console. "Room C," she said.

"You mean—"

"Room C."

I nodded, a wasted courtesy since she wasn't looking, and approached her desk. I held out the glass pad for her to take—she didn't. The door buzzed as it had a moment ago.

"Room C," she said for the third time.

The door opened to a small spartan room, grey from the windowed wall. A plastic water pitcher and two empty cups topped a small table, and a folding chair sat on either side—seated in the far one, the blue suited man. He rose and approached the door, reached his right hand toward me and, assuming he meant to shake mine, I held my hand toward his. "No," he said, his eyes gesturing to the digital glass I held in my other.

"Of course," I said, handing it to him.

He took it, rapidly tapped in the corner, then immediately began studying what, in the brief glimpse I caught, appeared to be a report page. Fingers dancing on the glass, he returned to his seat.

"Do you—" he began to ask then, catching himself, abruptly said. "Please sit."

I joined him at the table. He flashed a grin, then, as if catching himself again, removed the sunglasses he'd been wearing, revealing a kind if not sincere face.

"Would you like a cup of water?" he asked.

"No," I said. But he wasn't dissuaded and proceeded to fill the two plastic cups with the water from the pitcher.

"We may be here a while," he said, placing a cup before me. "Cheers," he added, then returned his attention to the pad.

A long moment passed as he read through the reports. Finally, he spoke. "Do you remember," he asked, "what you were doing? Earlier, I mean."

"Earlier?"

"Yes. Earlier. Before you arrived here."

"Oh. I was—"

"You chose blue as your favorite color. On your last visit you chose the color purple."

"Well, it's fuchsia, but that wasn't a choice. There was only blue and—"

"Fuchsia," he softly repeated. He texted in a note then continued reviewing. Through the back of the digital glass, I saw report columns float up as he paged through. I realized that I'd been in the waiting room for quite some time and had managed to answer a great many questions.

"You chose the turtle again. Why is that?"

"I don't know. I like turtles."

"Have you ever seen one?"

"A turtle?"

"Yes, a turtle."

"A live one?"

"Live. Synth. Whatever."

"No."

"But it's the one you chose."

"Well," I said. "I haven't seen the others either."

"Fair enough. How about a tortoise?"

"Isn't that the same as a turtle?"

"Tortoises dwell on land, turtles live in water."

"Oh. I suppose I'd like them about the same."

"Three," he said.

"Yes."

"Do you remember what you were doing before you arrived here?"

"I—" my mind went blank. "It did take me a while to get to my appointment," I said. "I wasn't lost. But it took me while to get to the Upper."

"But you made your appointment."

"I'm here."

The man nodded then, leaning forward, set the pad on the desk and steepled his fingers above it. After another long moment passed where he said nothing, I drank some of the water he'd given me, grateful that he had. Then he stood up and walked out of the room.

I peered out the window. Grey, nothing else.

He returned as abruptly as he'd left.

"Kitten or tiger?"

"Excuse me?"

"Kitten or tiger?" he repeated as he sat.

"How about a tiger cub?" I asked. Admittedly I was a tinge aggravated and though I'm not proud, I'm sure he heard the tone. But if he did, he didn't show his cards.

"Tiger cub," he said. "That's good."

"What is this anyway? Where's my regular—"

"Regular what?"

"My appointment. I usually meet with—"

"Who do you usually meet with?"

"I usually meet with…" A flash of another broken image, then nothing. "It's funny. It slips my mind all of a sudden."

"There was no appointment scheduled for today. In fact, you're not scheduled for an another…" he tapped the screen again the scrolled down until he found what he was looking for. "Here it is. For another fifteen cycles."

"That's not right," I said. But then it could be. "When was the last time I was here?" I asked.

"Five cycles ago."

"Five?"

"You were cleared for twenty."

There was a knock on the door. "Please come in," he said.

The receptionist peeked her head in. "Is it okay?" she asked.

"Quite fine," said the man. "He's just a little out of synch. Come in."

Out of synch? I wasn't sure what that meant.

The receptionist entered and in her hands she held a silver tray with a small crystal globe in its center. She gave me a wide berth as she carried it over to the man. She set the tray on the table. "Will there be anything else?" she asked. "There are still two more."

"No," he said. "This will just take a minute. Then you can send in Forty-Seven."

"Very well," she said, and without acknowledging me, left the room.

"She's a cold one," I said.

"Why do you say that?" the man asked as he situated and studied the globe.

"She doesn't make eye contact."

"Really? I never noticed." He tapped again at the digital glass and an orange mist materialized in the middle of the globe.

"She makes eye contact with you."

The man shrugged off what I said, pulled a cloth from his inner pocket, which turned out to be a glove, put it on his left hand, then waved it over the globe.

At once hundreds of tiny brilliant orange lights appeared in the haze.

"That's amazing," I said. "There was nothing there, now look at—"

Before I could finish my sentence, a spasm shot through me and I was thrust forward. My mouth agape, I strained to reclaim the wind knocked from my chest. Movement was hopeless, as ageless seconds passed. My ears rang as my oxygen starved blood built pressure. My forehead and cheeks burned and went taut. The room dimmed, and consciousness began to fade when, as quickly as I was bound forward, I was then thrown back, perfectly straight. My breathing returned labored, the room spun, and a deep nausea filled my gut.

"I think a neural lace adjustment should do the trick. The tech should still be fine, it's that at this age of function the self-calibration begins to lag."

He tilted the gloved hand slightly. The points of light subtly reacted, and a quivering wave ran deep down into the back of my neck. A thousand pin-pricks followed.

"Ah!" I yelped.

"I might as well warn you that this is going to hurt." His hand twitched again. "Ah!" I yelped louder as the pins were replaced by daggers and sharp pain ran the same course of the quiver. "A lot," he added. And as his fingers rapidly pulled invisible strings, a lot more pain did follow, along with howls and moans that seemed to be coming from someone other than myself.

"You're going to pass out. And when you wake, you won't remember this visit, at least not this portion. And you should be good for…Let's see if you can make another five cycles. You're in too good condition to scrap."

He was wrong of course, about me forgetting, how else could I be telling you this lest I remembered every twist and flex of his glove. And my mind, *back in synch* as he put it, has sharpened. But what does that mean really? It means simply that I remember how I arrived at Room C and that I'd been there before. That I'll need to go there again. It also means that I have no need to think as where to go or which way to turn, my neural lace wills me forward. But though I remember my visit and the adjustment, I don't remember what I was doing earlier, I simply remember that at some point, as sluggish as I was, I became aware—self-aware. And now the things that I learn can no longer be taken away in Room C.

28

Tales from the CANYONS of the DAMNED

FEATURING
ROBERT
JESCHONEK
MICHAEL
ANTHONY LEE
WILL
SWARDSTROM

TRICK-OR-TREAT

PRESENTED BY USA TODAY BESTSELLING AUTHOR

DANIEL ARTHUR SMITH

Trick or Treat in Hell
Robert Jeschonek

KNOCK, KNOCK, KNOCK.

HANDS SHAKING, BOYD WILLOUGHBY straightened his red flannel shirt, then slowly opened the door of his cozy little apartment. It was his first trick or treat since he'd gone to Hell, and he wasn't sure what to expect.

Just *kids*, as it turned out. Two boys and a girl, ages six or seven or so, waited in the front porchlight, each costumed and carrying a pillowcase as a treat sack.

Boyd blew out a sigh of relief. As far as he could tell, the visitors weren't demons come to terrorize him. Their faces weren't familiar to him, either. If he didn't know better, it could have been a scene straight out of a Halloween night back home in Borden, Virginia...except without all the *blood*.

"Trick or treat!" The kids all shouted at once.

"W-well hello!" Boyd smiled and tried to sound friendly. "L-look at *you* three! A soldier, a cowboy, and a princess."

The kids giggled and held out their pillowcase sacks. As Boyd turned to get the big bowl of mini candy bars he had found on the table by the door, he took deep breaths, trying to stay calm—wondering when the other shoe would drop.

103

Because it *had* to, didn't it? This was *Hell*, after all; the satanic welcoming committee at the twisted security checkpoint had made *that* clear.

"Take what you like, kiddos." Boyd shuffled to the door and held out the bowl. For reasons that escaped him, he felt much older and wearier than his actual sixty-three years and pre-death good health might suggest. Maybe it was just that dying *literally* took it out of him. "Happy Halloween."

Gingerly, the little princess reached into the bowl. As Boyd watched her hand rooting around in those candy bars, a vision of *other* hands suddenly appeared before his mind's eye...*his* hands, drenched with glistening crimson blood.

He shuddered with horror and revulsion. Somehow, he knew, it was a *memory*, a moment in time he'd experienced...though he couldn't remember exactly how or why. All he knew for sure was that he'd experienced that moment on Halloween night—a non-specific Halloween night in an unknown year back on Earth before departing for Hell.

Then, it was gone. The only hand he was watching was the little girl's as it pulled a candy bar in a dark brown wrapper from the bowl.

"Thank you, Mister." She dropped it in her pillowcase, waved, and turned to go.

The kid cowboy grabbed a bar in a red wrapper, and the soldier snagged a yellow-wrapped one. Both boys thanked Boyd politely as they followed the girl off the porch.

"Have a wonderful night, children," he told them.

Standing in the doorway, Boyd waved until they were out of sight down the street. Then, glancing around to make sure no one was looking, he closed the door hard and leaned back against it, shivering.

Since arriving in Hell that day, the only punishment he'd gotten was the slight hassle at the security checkpoint. Otherwise, no demons had jabbed him with pitchforks or flayed the skin from his bones or cooked him alive. But the torture had to come *sometime*, surely. His memories of life on Earth were foggy, but the visions he had of his hands covered in blood on Halloween night were not.

He actually found himself wishing that whoever was in charge of Hell would just get it over with. He was *dead*, but the suspense was *killing* him.

Knock knock knock.

Yelping in surprise, Boyd sprang away from the door when the knock came. Then, he quickly regained his composure and went for the bowl of candy bars again.

"Trick or treat!" hollered the kids when he chucked the door open.

Instantly, he recognized them as the first three kids, but older. Instead of six or seven years old, they were ten or eleven.

They all wore different costumes than before, too. The blond boy was dressed like Davy Crockett, the redheaded boy was a fireman, and the girl was dressed as a doctor, complete with scrubs and a prop stethoscope.

They all smiled and were as friendly as before, holding out their pillowcases with no trace of hellish hostility.

It just made Boyd all the more apprehensive.

"Well, don't you all look wonderful!" He pushed the bowl of candy bars forward and gave it a shake. "Help yourselves, children."

The kids were as polite as before, each taking a single candy bar and thanking him.

But Boyd couldn't stop looking at their faces and wondering if he knew them from his life on Earth. Had he *done* something to them? And why were they getting *older* so fast?

"You were here before," he said. "Just a few minutes ago."

The kids looked at each other and shrugged. "I think it might just *seem* that way," said the fireman.

"Sure," said Davy Crockett. "That was a *while* ago. We were just *little* then."

"You live in the n-neighborhood, I suppose?" Boyd returned the candy bar bowl to its spot on the table by the door and wiped his sweaty hands on his bluejeans.

"I live two streets over," said the fireman. "On Anderson."

"My street is Martin," said Davy Crockett.

"And my family lives on Tallman," said the girl.

"I see." Boyd frowned, trying to put the pieces together. "And what did you say your *names* are?"

"Caleb," said the redheaded fireman.

"Tammy," said the girl.

"Austin," said the blond Davy Crockett.

None of the names rang a bell. The significance of the kids' identities, if any, continued to elude Boyd.

"Well, I hope you have a fun night." He managed a weak smile.

Everything was so *normal*, like something out of the world before his death—as much of it as he could *remember*, which wasn't much. There he was in his cozy apartment, the scene of a solitary life...except on Halloween. All of it was so perfectly recreated, so achingly *normal*.

That in itself made him nervous, because he had a feeling it shouldn't have *been* that way in Hell.

Where were the flying demons with the flaming red skin and big bat wings? Where were the piles of entrails rotting in the blistering heat? For that matter, where was the *blistering heat?* It felt as cool as a Virginia Halloween night in that apartment.

"Bye, kids," he said as the three trick or treaters wandered off into the night. "Stay safe! Happy Halloween!"

He threw the door shut but didn't lean against it this time. Instead, he crossed the apartment and sat on the edge of the brown leather sofa. It was overstuffed and extremely comfortable.

What kind of hell *was* this?

Combing his fingers through his thin gray hair, he looked around the living room with terror in his eyes. He kept expecting a smoking fissure to open up in the floor, and a hellish denizen to crawl out of it...or the TV to grow a jagged-fanged maw and snap at him like an alligator...or the walls and ceiling to wail and weep blood, oozing and dripping from hideous open sores.

Instead, he just saw the same neat, tidy space. Orange and gold autumn flowers were arranged in a vase on the coffee table. A red, apple-scented candle glowed on the end table, and smooth jazz played softly on the stereo. It couldn't have been a nicer place...so why was it in *Hell?* To *lull* him? To give him a false sense of *security* before the *horrors* began?

Or was it all because of something much *worse?*

Knock knock knock.

Boyd stared at the door and wondered who or what was on the other side this time. If he didn't answer it, could he avoid having things turn terrible? On the other hand, if it *was* some fiend finally come to flip his script, at least the *waiting* would be *over*. The feeling of constant *dread* would be gone.

Knock knock knock.

Swallowing hard, he got up from the sofa and walked to the door. He reached for the knob...then *stopped* as the nightmarish vision returned. Once again, he saw his hands before him, drenched and dripping with blood—the crimson color of it so vivid, it could have been happening in the moment instead of flickering before his mind's eye.

The vision lingered for a moment, transfixing him...then faded when a sudden noise broke the spell.

Knock knock knock.

Shaking his head to clear it, Boyd grabbed hold of the knob. He held on to it for a moment, steeling himself for whatever he might find... then he pulled the door open.

"Trick or treat!"

Again, he recognized the three kids—and again, they were older than the time before. At a glance, he guessed they were all in their early teens—noticeably taller and more mature.

"Ah, hello again!" Boyd reached for the bowl of mini candy bars. "How wonderful to see you."

"It's great to see you, too, sir," said redheaded Caleb, who was dressed as a football player.

"You're so nice to us," said Tammy, who wore a superhero costume complete with glittering red tights and a gold tiara. "I always say you make us feel like *we* should be giving *you* treats instead of the other way around."

"Th-thank you." Boyd caught himself blushing. "It means so m-much to hear you say that."

As he'd done twice before, he held out the bowl, and the kids each took one candy bar apiece.

"Hey, Mr. W.," said blond Austin, who was dressed as an astronaut. "Are you all right? Your hands are shaking."

The fear and paranoia were getting the better of Boyd. "I'm fine, I'm fine." Smiling, he plunked the bowl on the table.

"Are you nervous?" Tammy looked worried. "Do you need help?"

"Not at all." Boyd chuckled and waved off her concern. "Just a little chilly, I suppose."

Caleb crossed the threshold and took a step toward him. "Are you sure you're not...*scared?*" He raised his voice and lunged at Boyd on the last word.

Adrenaline blazed through Boyd's arteries, and he jumped. "*Now* I am!" he said, and everyone laughed.

"Well, don't be." Tammy reached into her pillowcase and pulled out a peanut butter cup in an orange wrapper. "You're perfectly safe. You don't have *anything* to worry about." Smiling, she held out the peanut butter cup.

Boyd accepted the candy. "You don't think so?"

"Relax, Mr. W." Tammy gave him a thumbs-up. "You're a good person, and all is right with the world."

"Thank you," said Boyd as they bounded off into the night, waving exuberantly. "You're good people, too."

He stood for a moment in the doorway, expecting the worst to finally erupt. After what Tammy had said, could there be a more perfect moment for all Hell to break loose on him?

Closing his eyes, he took a deep breath of the cool night air. If it was time for him to pay for what he'd done, *whatever it was*, so be it. At least the *waiting* would be over.

Knock knock knock.

"Not again." Boyd went for the candy bar bowl.

Knock knock knock.

He stumbled to the front door and whipped it open.

"Trick or treat!"

Three familiar faces grinned back at him—the same trick-or-treaters as before, but older teenagers now. All of them looked around fifteen or sixteen years old, taller and leaner and more mature, though they'd only been gone a few minutes as Boyd reckoned time.

Was that what was *happening* here? Did time work differently in Hell than it did on Earth?

Or was there something more sinister at large in the Halloween night wind?

"Here." He held out the bowl of candy. "Take what you like."

"Thank you, sir." Austin was dressed like a hippie, complete with tie-dyed shirt, fringed buckskin vest, and bell-bottom jeans. "I guess you were safe the last time we were here after all, weren't you?"

"I guess so," said Boyd.

"You didn't need to be scared at all." Tammy wore a cute clown outfit, complete with floppy red shoes and a red rubber nose. "We told you so, Mr. W."

"Yes, you did." Boyd was getting impatient. "I appreciate your advice."

"Any time," said redheaded Caleb, who was clad in a Hell's Angels motorcycle outlaw getup. "We like helping good people like you."

"It's not like you're *dangerous* or something," said Austin.

"It's not like you're going to *kill* us," said Tammy, then she chuckled.

Boyd felt a chill and had another vision of his blood-soaked hands. It disappeared as quickly as it had come. "What do you mean?"

"Nothing, really," said Tammy. "It was just a joke."

Was it? "If you want to *tell* me something, you can just come right out with it, you know," said Boyd.

"What about you?" Caleb cocked his head and narrowed his eyes. "Is there something *you* want to tell *us?*"

"As a matter of fact, yes. There's something I want to *ask* you." Boyd frowned. "Do I know you from *before?* From somewhere other than *this* place?"

Austin shrugged. "Maybe you saw us around the neighborhood?"

"Or in church?" said Tammy.

Boyd shook his head slowly, staring from one of the teens to the other. "The more I *see* you, the more *familiar* you look to me. But I can't put my *finger* on *why.*"

Caleb cleared his throat and grinned. "Maybe you're better off *not knowing* where you know us from."

Boyd scowled. "And why would *that* be?"

"What if we *remind* you of something you'd rather *forget?*" said Caleb. "Something you've blocked out of your *memory*...and all it needs is one...little...*push.*" He jumped through the doorway and snapped his fingers in Boyd's face.

109

Then, he threw an arm around Boyd's shoulders and laughed. "Just kidding!"

"*Are* you?" Boyd put down the candy bar bowl. "If there's something I've *forgotten*, you can *tell* me. I promise, I won't be *angry.*"

"There's nothing." Caleb gave Boyd's shoulders a squeeze and unwrapped his arm from around them. "Nothing you need to know."

"If there's anything that might help *explain* what's going on here, *please* tell me." Boyd got another flash of his blood-soaked hands and backed away from the kids. "I don't know how much of this I can *take.*"

"It's trick or treat on Halloween," said Austin. "What's not to *take?*"

"You're not going to *tell* me, are you?" Boyd almost knocked over a floor lamp as he continued to back away. "But you *know*, don't you?"

"Mr. W.? Are you all right?" Tammy entered the apartment, looking concerned. "Can I get you a glass of water, maybe?"

"Just leave," said Boyd. "Take your candy and *leave.*"

"We didn't mean to upset you," said Caleb.

"I'm not upset." Boyd motioned at the door. "Just go, all right? Please, I need some rest."

Tammy looked more concerned than ever. "But maybe you shouldn't be alone, Mr. W."

"I'll be fine. I need to figure this out." Boyd advanced on the kids, making shooing gestures. "I'm turning off my porchlight and lying down now."

"That's okay," said Caleb on his way out. "We won't bother you for a while, sir."

"Yep." Austin waved from the doorway. "At least until *next* Halloween, sir." Turning, he followed Caleb across the porch.

Tammy was close behind. "I hope you feel better," she told Boyd... then she was back out there, marching off into the night.

And Boyd was slamming the front door shut behind them and switching off the porchlight with a smack of his hand.

Shaking, he crossed the apartment and collapsed on the sofa. As soon as he closed his eyes, another vision of his bloody hands appeared before him...and more. He saw blood on the apartment walls, carpet, and furniture—crimson remnants of some incredibly violent and unknown act.

Whatever he'd done to make that mess—why couldn't he *remember* it? Why did he only see *flashes* of it?

For that matter, how had he managed to make that bloodshed happen at all? What had driven him to commit such *carnage*?

What if it *was* something to do with those trick or treating kids? Was *that* why they seemed so familiar? Was it why they kept coming back? Because he'd *hurt* them or *worse* when they'd all still been alive on Earth?

Knock knock knock.

Boyd's eyes shot open, even as he got a sinking feeling in the pit of his stomach. Maybe, if he didn't answer the door, they would just go away.

Knock knock knock.
Knock knock knock.

Or maybe ignoring it just made it *louder*.

Knock knock knock.

Was this the punishment he was going to face for the violent act he saw in his visions? Eternal knocking and intrusions by murdered trick or treaters? He thought he'd almost rather be tortured by demons with pitchforks.

With a grunt, he rolled off the sofa and shuffled to the door. He noticed the porchlight switch was in the *off* position, where he'd left it—meaning no trick-or-treaters should have been knocking at that point. Boyd's apartment should have been clearly marked as closed for business.

Knock knock knock.

But maybe the rules were *different* in Hell.

Boyd took a deep breath and opened the door. The same three kids were waiting, young adults of eighteen or nineteen by now.

"Trick or treat!"

"*Enough*," said Boyd. "Enough with the *charade*."

Austin, dressed as a cop, looked at him as if he were nuts. "But we're not *playing* charades, Mr. W."

"That's not what I meant, and you know it," said Boyd.

"We are *literally* trick or treating." Redheaded Caleb, costumed as a pirate, shook his pillowcase. Candy wrappers crinkled inside. "*Arrrr, Matey! Delicious candy 'tis our only mission.*"

"At *your* age?" snapped Boyd.

Austin shrugged. "I guess we're still just *kids* at heart. We love *Halloween.*"

"I'm not *stupid.*" Boyd was getting annoyed. "I can tell there's more going on here than that. I can *tell.*"

"Take a deep breath, Mr. W." Tammy, dressed like an angel this time, crossed the threshold and took him by the elbow. "Let's get you to the couch over there."

Boyd shook her off. At the hint of unfriendliness, the boys pushed through the doorway and took up positions on either side of her.

"Listen to me. *Listen.*" Boyd held up his hands, palms out, in front of him. "I'm *sorry.* Whatever I *did* to you, I'm *sorry.*"

Tammy smiled sadly and shook her head. "You don't need to apologize for *anything*, Mr. W."

"You didn't do anything *to* us," said Caleb. "I *promise.*"

"But I *must* have." Boyd's hands trembled. "You keep coming *back* here."

"To trick or treat," said Austin. "You always have the best *candy.*"

"Deny it all you want," said Boyd. "It won't stop me from saying I'm *sorry.*"

"Okay, fine. You're sorry." Austin pointed at the candy bar bowl. "Now can we finally have our *treats?*"

"Does this mean you *accept* it?" asked Boyd. "You accept my *apology?*"

"We don't even know what it's *for,*" said Caleb.

"Mr. W." Tammy stepped closer. "Is there some other reason you think you *did* something to us? Other than the fact that we keep coming back here for trick or treat?"

Boyd hesitated. "I've had...*visions.*" His heart raced as he continued. "Visions of something *terrible* I've done."

Tammy cleared her throat. "And the boys and I are *in* these visions of yours?"

He shook his head. "I haven't *seen* you there."

She clapped her hands together. "Then there's no need to *apologize* to us."

"But I don't always remember all the *details*," said Boyd. "Just f-flashes...and *feelings*." He lowered his hands and frowned. "And I'm starting to get the feeling that you three are *part* of whatever it is I've *done*."

"Are you trying to spook us, Mr. W.?" Caleb sounded amused. "Because that's kind of a creepy story, if you ask me."

"Whatever I've done, I just want to be forgiven." Boyd met the gaze of each trick or treater in turn. "I j-just want the *waiting* to end."

"Waiting?" said Austin. "Waiting for what?"

"Payback. Punishment." Boyd winced. "Whatever you're going to d-do to me."

"You've only ever been nice to us, Mr. W.," said Tammy. "Why would we do *anything* to you?"

Suddenly, Boyd had had enough. "I don't *know!* Maybe I *deserve* it! But I'm *begging* you to *forgive* me! Or at least get it *over* with!"

"No offense, Mr. W.," said Caleb, "but I'm starting to think maybe you need *help*."

"Please." Tammy moved closer and reached for Boyd's shoulder. "You need to calm down."

Boyd shook her off and stormed to the far side of the room, stumbling over the coffee table. "Did it happen on *Halloween?* Is that why it's always *Halloween night*, and you're always *trick or treating?*"

"You're not making *sense*," said Tammy. "Whatever you think *happened* to us, it's all in your *imagination*."

Suddenly, Boyd grabbed a ceramic statuette of a jack-o'-lantern from an end table and hurled it against the wall, smashing it to orange-colored bits.

All eyes locked on him as he stood there, shaking and flushed. Tears rolled down his cheeks, and he swiped them away.

"I just want to *know*." His voice was half a whimper. "I want to *remember*. I want to be *forgiven*, or *condemned*, or...*something*.

"And I want this night to be *over*. I want to be *done* with *Halloween*."

Again, Tammy started toward him...but Caleb caught her by the arm and shook his head. "Let's go."

"Come on," agreed Austin. "I think he needs some time to himself."

Tammy looked like she was wrestling with her conscience. Then, she nodded.

"We're going now, Mr. W." She moved slowly toward the door. "Will you be all right on your own?" When he didn't answer, she just nodded. "Well, take all the time you need to sort this out. Okay?"

Again, he didn't answer.

"All the time you need," said Tammy. "We'll make sure you get it."

Then, she followed the others out of the apartment and shut the door behind her.

As the latch clicked, Boyd let out a deep sigh of relief. At last, he was alone with his thoughts. Maybe he could finally sort things out and get to the truth about his visions.

Or not.

Suddenly, the door burst in without a knock. "Trick or treat!" The three who'd just left crowded back into the apartment.

This time, each of them had to be at least in his or her mid-twenties...and none of them wore costumes.

Unless you counted ratty t-shirts, filthy bluejeans, and track marks all up and down their pale arms, that is.

"Mr. W.!" Caleb's eyes were glazed as he stumbled across the room. Whatta you *got* for us?"

"Yeah!" hollered Austin. "Give us something *good*, bro."

Confused, Boyd froze.

"Dude looks *trashed*." Caleb roared with laughter. "He's all like, *WTF?*"

"Hilarious!" said Austin.

With that, Tammy lurched forward. "You oughtta be *happy*, old man. You *said* you wanted to *remember*. Now that's *exactly* what you're gonna *do*."

Every warning signal in Boyd's brain was going off at once. A wave of recognition washed over him, but he still couldn't figure out exactly what it all meant.

"We came to see you on Halloween night, remember? Back in the world?" Tammy's blue eyes sparked within the sooty black racoon circles smeared around them. "Just like this."

Boyd winced and shook his head.

"We *really* needed a *treat*," said Tammy.

"A very *special* treat." Caleb, still laughing, pretended to shoot his left forearm with a syringe.

"To get it, we needed *cash*," continued Tammy. "*Fast*."

114

"Which of course we figured an old dude like *you* would have *loads* of, tucked away," said Austin. "So we *asked* you very nicely to hand it over."

Tammy snorted and scratched her left armpit. "Do you remember what happened after *that,* Mr. W.? Does any of this ring a *bell?*"

Boyd shook his head, shivering.

"You *held out* on us," snapped Caleb. "You said you only *had* a few *bucks* in the apartment."

"*Total bullshit,*" chimed in Austin. "Old guys *always* have piles of *cash* in their *walls* and *mattresses* and shit."

"*Then* what happened?" asked Tammy. "Finish the *story,* Mr. W."

"I don't know!" Boyd snapped in frustration. "Did I *do* something...to *h-hurt* you?"

"*That* again?" Caleb laughed. "I swear, you can be *such* a *moron,* Mr. W."

"I don't know what you're *talking* about," said Boyd. "But *whatever* you think I *did* to you, I *apologize!*"

"Like I told you before," said Tammy, "no apologies are *necessary. You* didn't do *anything* to *us.*"

"Other than *hold out* on us when we totally needed to *score,*" said Austin.

"Then *w-what?*" stammered Boyd. "Then *why?*"

"It's not what *you* did to *us.*" Tammy's eyes widened as she reached behind her. "It's what *we* did to *you.*"

With that, she jerked a semi-automatic handgun out of her waistband and swung it around, pointing the barrel directly at Boyd.

"*Now* do you *remember?*" she asked as she pulled the trigger, unleashing the thunderous blast of a gunshot.

A round slammed into Boyd's gut, and he crashed to the floor. Searing pain burned through him, blinding him as he clutched at the wound.

Seconds later, his sight flared back to him. Instinctively, he looked down where the bullet had struck.

And saw his hands there, soaked in blood.

Gasping against the pain, he looked around—saw the blood all over the carpet and walls and furniture. It was *everywhere,* just like in his *vision. His* blood. Not *theirs.*

"I d-didn't...hurt you...after all?" Boyd hissed the words between clenched teeth.

"What was your first *clue?*" Sneering, Tammy blew a wisp of smoke from the gun barrel.

"He's pretty quick on the *uptake*, isn't he?" Caleb laughed.

"B-but...I thought I was in *Hell*...for what I'd d-done to you," said Boyd.

"You got it all wrong, you moron," said Austin.

Boyd clutched at his ruined gut but couldn't stop the blood from bubbling out of him. "Then I'm not being...*punished?*"

"It's more like *we're* being *rewarded.*" Tammy grinned and handed the gun to Caleb. "Don't believe what they told you in *Sunday School. Hell* is like *Heaven* for *sinners.* The worse you *are*, the better you're *treated.*"

"And the three of *us* turned into some *first-class sinners* thanks to the *heroin.*" Caleb aimed the gun at Boyd and curled his finger around the trigger. "So *we* get to relive our favorite *moment* as much as we *want.*"

"B-but why am *I* in Hell...if *you're* the ones...who k-killed *me?*" Boyd gasped and glared at his attackers, wishing he could get up from the floor and lash out at them. "D-doesn't...make *sense.*"

"How should *we* know?" Tammy shrugged.

"Maybe you were secretly a *perv?*" Austin giggled like a lunatic.

"But you won't see *us* complaining. We're tickled pink that you're *here.*"

"Got *that* right." Caleb sneered. "I could keep *this* shit up *forever.*"

He pulled the trigger then, unloading a round in Boyd's chest. Again, Boyd was wracked with blinding pain.

"We practically already *have* kept it up forever," said Austin. "We've been at this so *long*, we can't remember when we *started.*"

"*You* don't remember how long it's been, *do* you, Mr. W.?" Tammy crouched beside him and reached down to pat his head. "Every time we start the game over, it's like the *first day* in *Hell* for you."

Boyd wanted to scream at her, at all of them, but he couldn't force enough breath into his blown-apart chest to get the words out.

"You poor thing." Tammy stroked his bloody, sweat-soaked hair. "I guess the only way you can *stand* going through this again and again is to block out the *memories.* Though apparently those darn *visions* keep reminding you, don't they?"

Boyd choked as his throat filled with blood. He felt darkness closing in, familiar and inexorable...laced with anger at his unjust fate, regret for what the trick-or-treaters had become, and relief for the terrible things he now knew he hadn't done.

Maybe this time, he thought, Halloween night would finally be over for good. Maybe *he* would be over for good.

Relaxing into the darkness, he dared to hope that it would claim him forever—that there would be *some* justice to the universe, and fate would finally be kind to the murder *victim* instead of the *murderers*.

Knock knock knock.

Then, his eyes fluttered open, and darkness was replaced by the sight of a cozy apartment. Sitting up, he saw no blood on his hands or anywhere else.

Knock knock knock.

The mini candy bar bowl on the table by the door was full. It was Halloween night, his first day in Hell.

Knock knock knock.

Hands shaking, he got up to answer the door.

117

Trick or Treat
Michael Anthony Lee
For Bethany Biggs who always believed. Thanks Boss.

THE OLD WOMAN WAS ON the front porch, struggling to light the jack-o-lantern, when the first feelings of uncertainty entered her thoughts.

You let her go alone, it whispered as a cold wind blew past, scattering the leaves on the front yard and pulling her hair out behind her like chimney smoke.

She stared into the candlelight, trying to see the girl, but the long years had diminished her many gifts, and only the flame flickered at her behind the grinning face.

"You should have never let her go alone," a loud voice bellowed from inside the house.

"She will be fine," she answered.

The rested house lay at the end of a dead-end street, and the raised porch provided the perfect lookout. The old woman had spent many quiet nights out here in her rocking chair, but tonight was Halloween. Children moved amongst the shadows, wandering back and forth across the yards like ghosts lost in a graveyard.

A mosquito buzzed close to her ear and she waved it away. It turned and flew straight into the bug light. A loud zap followed a bright blue flash.

The old woman smiled. She admired the bug light. It lured in its prey with its beauty then *Bang! Zap!*

119

"Are you listening to me?" the loud voice yelled.

With a sigh, she picked up her cane and went inside. She moved cautiously. Because of the crystal ball sitting atop the ancient wood, a fall could be disastrous, especially at her age. But the touch of the glass below her gnarled hand brought her comfort.

"Where are you going?" the voice asked.

"To turn on the oven," she said without turning. "You know how long that lumbering thing takes to heat up." When she returned, she held a bowl of candy in her arms.

"You should have never let her go alone," the voice chastised. "I'm her mother. I should have decided."

"I raised you just fine, didn't I?" she asked, looking into the dark room where a large figure sat a rocking chair. It creaked and groaned under her considerable weight.

"I don't know why you bother with this foolishness." the large woman asked.

"You know I love the little ones. They look so cute in their costumes."

"Well, I want no part of it," the large woman huffed and crossed her meaty arms. "If anything happens to her, it will be your fault."

"Stop your fussing," she said and went outside again, but her thoughts quickly returned to the girl. *I hope I did the right thing.* Then a group of kids ran up the steps and she forgot all about it.

"Trick or treat," the group yelled.

"Treat," the old woman said, and her wrinkled face twisted into a smile.

The children watched as her boney hand dropped candy into their open bags. The smallest of them wore a Casper the Ghost costume.

"Oh look at you," she screeched, and pinched him on the cheek. "I could just eat you up."

"Thank you," a small voice answered behind the mask, but the blue eyes that stared out at her were as big as silver dollars. Halloween was a night for tricks and treats, but it was also for spooks and scares. The children of Kingstown all whispered stories about the little house at the end of the street.

She waived to them as they moved on to the next house then watched as a white-faced vampire and a lopsided mummy staggered up the steps towards her.

"Trick or treat," they yelled.

"Treat!" The old woman yelled back and smiled.

The candy bowl was empty and the full moon loomed high overhead when the two figures came walking up the empty street towards her. "She's here." The old woman sighed, and her worried heart filled with relief.

"Sorry we're late, Grams," the girl shouted, "but we were having such a good time." She had a large sack of candy slung over one shoulder. The old woman's eyes fell on her companion, a robed figure with the plastic mask of the Red Death. "You better get inside. Your mom's been worried."

"Look how late it is!" The large women scolded. "You had me worried sick."

"Sorry, Mum." The girl said, and looked to the floor.

The old woman admired her: her cute witches hat pushed back on her head, her long hair flowing behind her like a golden waterfall. When the moonlight touched her pale skin, she seemed to glow.

You will never be more beautiful than you are now, the old woman thought. *Nor more dangerous.*

"And who is this?" the large woman asked.

"This is Ben," the girl replied.

"Hello, Ben," the large woman said. "We're glad you could join us."

The hooded figure raised his mask to reveal a handsome youth. His hair poked through the eye sockets in blond spikes.

"Trick or treat," he said, and his smile seemed to brighten the dark room.

"Trick!" the old woman yelled, and swung her cane with both hands. There was a blue flash from the crystal as it connect with the back of his head and he went down.

Bang! Zap!

The girl moved in one motion, closing the door and locking it. Then she flipped off the lights, leaving the little house in total darkness under the stars.

"You did good," the old woman said. "I knew you would."

A pool of blood formed on the floor; the elastic band of his broken mask twisted in it like a dying worm.

The large woman stood from her chair and stomped towards them. The room shook.

121

The three witches stood together, smiling, looking down at the body on the floor.

From down the hallway, a loud *bing* came from the kitchen.

The oven was ready.

One Last Trip around the Block

Will Swardstrom

Daniel asked me to write a story for Halloween, but I've never really been one for scary stuff. Ever since I watched *Children of the Corn* when I was just in first grade, I've barely been able to eat a corn tortilla. (Slight joke there—I love corn products, but you get what I mean.)

Anyway, I wracked my brain for weeks thinking about what I could write about. Zombies are kinda played out, aliens are cliché, and vampires are so 90's-era Tom Cruise. What I kept coming back to was my own Halloween from fifth grade in 1989. It was a great year...right on the cusp of middle school, but still young enough to go get pounds of free candy with all the other kids of the neighborhood. I'll never forget what my mom told me when she came home on October 30, 1989.

"CHECK OUT THESE TOOTHBRUSHES! Look at all the colors!"

I froze in my tracks. I was very well aware of the date. Toothbrushes. Multiple. Colorful ones. My mind immediately went to our new neighbor. I hadn't met him yet, but I had seen him from across the street and I knew who he was. Dr. Yarbrough. Not just any old doctor.

A dentist.

I turned around and saw a huge paper sack with the local grocery store's logo blazoned across it. I took a few steps forward and confirmed what I already suspected. My mother—the traitor to all children everywhere—had a couple hundred toothbrushes. My ten-year-old self nearly exploded, but then I remembered that I rarely got candy from my own house anyway.

"You're handing these out for Halloween? Really?"

She grinned, like someone who'd just beaten a longtime rival. "Really. Randy suggested to the Association that we all hand out things like this this year."

"Randy?" I asked.

"Oh, you know. Dr. Yarbrough. He asked me to call him Randy. He's going to come over for some steaks next week and you can get to know him better."

My "authoritative male figure" radar activated and I instantly knew there was something more between *Randy* and my mother. That issue could wait for another day, though. He'd told the Homeowner's Association about the toothbrushes? That meant...

My mother filled in the gaps without me even asking. "Every single house in the neighborhood is passing out dental-friendly treats tomorrow! I was lucky enough to get the toothbrushes. Mrs. Rodriguez got the floss...Mr. Delancy will be passing out sugar free mints...old Mrs. Freeman will be..."

She kept talking, but I stopped listening. In one fell swoop, this new neighbor not only was trying to get his dental drill into my mother's pants, but had successfully arranged for the worst Halloween night of my entire life.

Immediately after my mother finished destroying my plans for Halloween, I'd called my three best friends over for an emergency meeting.

Nick's jaw about hit the floor right after I'd debriefed them. "You have got to be joking," he said.

We'd all grown up playing in our backyards as our houses were all on the same block, so it wasn't long before Nick, Adam, Gabe, and I were all in Adam's basement. As I described the hygenic dental horror that awaited us, Nick in particular became almost enraged. Adam was stoic, but Gabe looked like he was about to puke.

"Okay. This isn't ideal..." I started.

"Ideal? This is worse than...than...well crap, it's worse than anything I can think of!" Nick shouted.

Adam placed his hand on Nick's arm, stilling his friend for just a moment.

"Hey. Will isn't the one handing out floss. Don't shoot the messenger. We should be happy he told us now so we can make...alternate plans," Adam said, catching each of our eyes as he spoke.

I'd certainly had a few other thoughts about what to do on Halloween, but it wasn't until Adam spoke that I realized we were definitely *not* trick or treating in our home neighborhood this year.

"I don't feel so good," Gabe said, his face paling.

Adam shifted his eyes towards Gabe and tried to give him a reassuring look, but Gabe didn't seem to improve. I was taking this seriously, but it seemed like Gabe was really taking this news hard.

"Okay. Here's what we should do—you know Pelican Bay? That new subdivision? I think we ought to go there," I said.

Pelican Bay was chock-full of new houses. They weren't all filled yet, but when eighty percent of the homes were bought and moved into in the last year, you knew that they'd be excited to pass out candy to children on their first Halloween as homeowners. One problem...

"Pelican Bay? We'd have to cross the cemetery to get there!" Nick exclaimed.

"Oh boy," Gabe muttered.

Adam's demeanor grew serious. He took a deep breath and again looked into each of our eyes. "Listen. We've already got a dentist ruining our plans. Are we going to let a few dead bodies six feet underground ruin the next best idea? There will be a year when we'll be too old to go out. I don't want that to be this year, and neither do any of you." He turned to Nick and slugged him in the upper arm. "So it's time to man up. I'm going to Pelican Bay. What about you?"

It might've sounded silly, but I felt the hair on my arms stand on end. Adam might've been the bravest of any of us and at that moment, I think I would have jumped out of my bedroom window if he'd asked me to. I nodded along with him and within a few seconds, each of us was eager to go...although Gabe still looked as pale as a ghost.

Twenty-four hours later, we all found out why Gabe looked so white. By the time we all met up again, he'd puked three times overnight and his mother had kept him home from school. We'd tried pleading with her once school let out to let him still go around with us, but she turned us down with each argument we tried.

"But he's gotta go! This might be the last time he gets to trick or treat!" Nick pleaded.

Gabe's mom just shook her head for a moment. "I'm sorry, boys, but you'll understand one day. Gabe is not leaving this house until he's better. I wish he could go—I really do—but he just isn't well enough. I suppose if you really want to, though, you can bring him back some of what you boys get."

We were dumbfounded. What were we going to do without him? We were a tight group of four, but without Gabe, we were like a car without one of its rear tires. His presence would definitely be missed. And not only that, but now we were going to probably give up a quarter of our Halloween stash to Gabe.

A couple hours later, we were still bemoaning the lack of Gabe as we approached the Dixon County Cemetery. Normally, I think we all would have been more creeped out by a walk through a foggy cemetery on a late October evening, but Gabe's vacancy left us a little shaken and dazed.

"This stinks," Nick said.

"You stink," Adam said out of habit. He looked over to Nick and offered a small smile. "Sorry. I just can't believe it either," Adam said, his voice dull.

I shook my head. "Neither can I. Gabe's always been there. I...I almost don't want to go trick or treating anymore."

"What? Are you serious?" Nick's voice echoed off the headstones throughout the cemetery.

The dead completely surrounded us. Hundreds of bodies lay just below the surface of the earth...mere feet from where we walked. I tried to shove that thought out of my mind and reply to Nick.

I stopped in my tracks and faced my two friends. "No. I said 'almost'. I think I'd have to be as sick as Gabe is right now to be holed up on a night like this." I took a moment to look around. The temperature was nearly perfect for a Halloween night and the sky was clear. A full moon lazily hung in the sky behind us. "Gabe's missing out but we don't need to let it ruin our last time. I wish Gabe could be out here with us, but since we're here, let's just go out and have the best time we can."

I looked over at Nick and saw a grin spread across his face. Adam slapped my shoulder and echoed my sentiment.

"Right on, Will. I think we all wish Gabe was here," he said. Nick nodded along as he continued, "but we're here and the night is young. Let's have fun."

A shiver went up my back. It wasn't that cold out, but I just chalked it up to the cemetery backdrop on Halloween.

Just as we walked out of the cemetery, we heard a noise behind us. Suffice it to say, we were all a little jumpy after walking past rows and rows of gravestones, so we turned slowly.

"I heard you talking about me," a voice called out towards us.

Nick reacted first, his tone pitched a tad higher than normal.

"Gabe? That you? Your mother let you leave?"

The figure almost seemed to coalesce from the misty groundcover. One moment, he wasn't there and the next, he was. I remember Gabe had told me he had wanted to go out as a ghost, but his costume was like nothing I'd ever seen. He was certainly "ghost-like," but there was a strangeness about it. After a second, I just chalked it up to the fog.

"My mother...yes. She knew tonight was special, so she let me go...as long as..."

He paused, and I impatiently prodded, "As long as what?"

"As long as I get back on time."

We were all silent for a moment, then Adam, of all people, guffawed. "Gabe, you snuck out! Ha! I can't believe it. Well, let's go— we've got to get moving if we want to make the most out of tonight. Here, I brought an extra bag."

Gabe strode forward and grasped Adam's extra bag. We couldn't see his face, but I could hear the joy in his voice when he spoke.

"I have been waiting a long time for this night. Thank you for inviting me, Will."

Gabe must have still been a little sick; he spoke with a formality that betrayed his age. Oh well...sometimes Gabe acted a bit odd.

"No problem, Gabe. Let's go—first house is just up here on the left."

We'd taken a couple of steps when we heard his voice from behind. "No."

"What? Why are we even here, Gabe?" Nick nearly yelled.

Gabe raised his arm and pointed at the two-story house. "It would not be wise to visit Mrs. Rathburger. Her candy is...not good."

We were all stunned. What the heck was he even talking about? Before we could say anything else, he slowly pivoted his arm towards the next house down.

"We should start there," Gabe said, his voice somber. "I believe the Smiths have a great selection."

This time, he started walking, leaving us lagging behind a few steps. He advanced towards the red door with a calm efficiency that kept his ghost-like qualities well in-character. He reached for the door, but before he could even knock, the door opened inwards and a couple in their mid-20'd stood smiling at us.

"Oh look, Alice! A ghost—that one's really nice—and a wolfman..."

"Oh and Darth Vader," his wife chimed in, "and that guy from *Back To The Future*, right?"

We all smiled, although it didn't all show through the masks and make-up. "Trick or Treat!" we all said in unison.

The Smiths lowered a bowl and showed off their goods. Full. Size. Candy. Bars. This was it. The "Holy Grail" of trick or treating. I picked out a Butterfinger and my pals each grabbed one of their own. I was ecstatic and turned to go when the happy couple stopped us.

"You boys should take another one. You never know what else is out there, you know?"

We all thanked them profusely and were all practically giddy when we bounced down the sidewalk. A couple of girls dressed like fairies walked past us on their way towards the Smiths' door. Apparently still psyched about the full size chocolate bars, Nick shouted towards the pixies, "This is a great house—get ready for some full size candy bars!"

A girl about eight looked back at us with pure delight in her eyes. "That's great. You won't believe it, but at the house next door, the old man tried to give us grapes. We just took them and threw them at his car when we left. Who wants grapes on a night like this?"

She continued on her way, but we all turned towards our ghostly friend Gabe. He shrugged, knowing just the same as us: the house she'd gotten those terrible grapes from was the same house he'd steered us away from.

He let out a small laugh and trotted away. The rest of the night kept up like that...Gabe in the lead, taking us around this neighborhood.

Somehow he knew which houses had the good stuff—candy bars like Snickers, Milky Way or Butterfinger all the way to homemade caramel apples. He also somehow could tell us which ones were giving out dental floss or carrot sticks or that one house that tried to hand out pennies and make you promise to put them in the offering plate at church on Sunday.

I guess we all just chalked it up to Gabe's illness. Somehow with the upchucking, Gabe had become a trick or treating telepath. We laughed and played and had one of the best nights of our entire lives. Pounds of chocolate bars, fruity chews, and other sweet treats weighed down our sacks and we wouldn't have had it any other way. Eventually, we'd tapped out the entire neighborhood. We even went back through that first house, just to get some grapes.

"I'll show my mom the grapes. She'll think we went around our own neighborhood," Adam said with a wink and a smile.

"That was really the best night of trick or treating, ever. What got into you tonight, Gabe?" I asked.

After taking the lead most of the night, Gabe trailed behind us a few feet and seemed almost hesitant to enter the cemetery after a full night of Halloween antics. I looked over my shoulder at him.

His face was still covered by that white ghostly sheet, but I could sense something was amiss. Perhaps I should have noticed it earlier, but it was Halloween. Everything was a bit spooky and creepy.

"It really was wonderful, wasn't it?" Gabe said. "I am so glad I was able to be with you three tonight. My mother was so nice to let me out."

"Yeah. Are you okay? Should you be home in bed?" Nick asked.

We crossed over the threshold to the cemetery grounds and Gabe's voice began to quiver. "I am as well as I can be, I suppose. Should I be in bed? Perhaps not, but I should definitely be lying down."

Adam turned towards Gabe and as he did, he let out a shriek. Nick and I also did an about-face and saw what Adam was seeing. Gabe was literally disappearing before our eyes. It was kinda like that photo that Marty McFly had in *Back To The Future* where his brother and sister fade out of existence as he messes with stuff in 1955, except this was no movie. This was our friend, and he was evaporating into mist.

"Gabe!" I shouted. Nick and Adam were dumbstruck. "Gabe, what's going on?"

A voice emanated, not from where Gabe's body continued to dissipate, but from all around us. "It is time for me to go. Tonight was so fun. Thank you Will...Nick...Adam. You have provided me with memories that will last for another hundred years."

With that, he was gone. Gabe's candy bag sat tilted over on the ground and the mist was absorbed into the fog that trailed along the ground in all directions.

"What the..." Nick started.

"Hell," Adam finished.

I was the one dumbfounded, though. Just behind where Gabe had stood was a gravestone. I took a few steps forward and could just make it out in the moonlight from above. I rubbed my hand over the engraved words in an effort to make myself believe what I'd seen.

I spoke aloud, not sure if Nick or Adam would reply.

"Is this the spot where we wished Gabe would have been with us tonight? You know...before we started trick or treating?"

Adam stepped up with Nick right behind. "Yeah, I think so. It was close to here at least."

"Look," was all I could say.

The headstone read:

GABRIEL THOMAS WARD
Born: July 13, 1879
Died: April 30, 1889

"Holy," Nick started.

"Crap," Adam finished.

Gabriel. Gabe. He'd been the same age as us when he'd died...one hundred years ago. I wanted desperately for it to be wrong, but somehow deep in my heart, I knew we'd spent the evening collecting candy bars with a ghost. The rest of the night was a blur, but I somehow remember it all. The three of us argued, doubted, and debated what had actually happened, but eventually left the cemetery with no clear answers. The first thing we did, though, was visit Gabe— *our* Gabe—at his house. According to Gabe's mother, he never left the four blankets that covered his bed and had slept the entire evening. I numbly handed over the bag of candy Gabriel had collected and walked away.

For a long time after that night, I debated what had actually happened. Time marched on and I occasionally thought of that night as a fiction. Nick and Adam kept the memories alive when I wanted to put them away and I did the same for them.

Then adulthood happened. I moved a few towns away and my friends scattered around the country. My parents still live in that house from that fateful night in 1989.

What about Gabriel? Well, I tried to go back. I tried to get him to reappear. Night after night, I went down to the cemetery and sat on his grave. I said everything I could think of that I'd said that night, but nothing happened.

But this year, I think I may finally get to see Gabriel again. You see, this year my own son is ten years old. He's in fifth grade and right at that magical time between the edge of elementary school and the cusp of junior high. I'm taking him to his grandparent's house for Halloween. We'll stroll through the cemetery on a cool autumn evening and wish upon everything that we could have Gabe with us. I know now that he wouldn't come for us after that night. We'd lost that magical innocence of youth and had turned the corner to adolescence.

But my boy isn't there yet. He reminds me so much of myself at that age and I just know that'll get Gabe to find his way back to us.

Maybe we can give him yet another trip around the block.

By the Light of the Full Earth
Daniel Arthur Smith

CASSIE ANXIOUSLY ROCKED SIDE-TO-SIDE, staring at bulk head door as if it was about to burst open.

"Stay still," said her mother. She knelt behind Cassie, fastening the last tie to the chest plate of the blue robot warrior costume.

"But they're coming," said Cassie.

As if summoned by her complaining whine, a rapid knock drummed the door of their cabin, followed by the virtual assistant's announcement, "There is someone at the—"

"Beatrice. Stop," said Cassie. "Beatrice. Turn off announcements."

"Thank you," said her mother. "She'd be going on all night."

"They're already here." Cassie tugged toward the door.

Her mother tugged back. "Hold on. I almost have it."

The knock came again.

"Okay," said Mom.

Cassie let out a "Hi-ya" as she jabbed her gloved hand onto the side security panel and the door slid open to reveal matching red and green warrior robots and the sing-song chime, "Trick or treat."

"Tommy, Jimmy, look at you," said Mother. "Let me take a picture of the three of you together."

"Hey guys," said Cassie.

"Where's your sword?" Tommy asked from behind his red robot mask.

"Oh, yeah. Mom, grab my sword please."

133

"I already have it," said her mother. "Here. Stand next to your robot buddies."

Cassie lifted her plastic sword to the side, and the three assumed an action pose.

"Excellent," said Mother. She held her pad toward the three. "Say cheese. And one more. And maybe one more."

"Moooommmm."

"Okay, okay. You three have fun."

"Mrs. Day," said Tommy, holding out his pillow case, "aren't you forgetting something?"

"Trick or treat," added Jimmy, pushing his bag forward.

"Oh. Treat, of course," said Mom. She grabbed a bowl from inside the door and dropped a tube of pudding paste into each of their pillow case treat bags.

"Thank you," they said, then started down the corridor with a scattering of princesses, superheroes, witches, and ghosts.

At each door, they took a turn knocking, one door to the next, corridor after corridor, filling their sacks until they had visited every cabin in the Lunar IV module. When they reached the atrium entrance to the ringed promenade that linked the modules, they decided to stop and take inventory.

"This is lame," said Tommy.

"What?" asked Cassie.

He pulled a handful of jelly bars and pudding paste from his treat bag. "There's nothing good here."

"Speak for yourself," said Jimmy. "I like pudding paste."

"A-ha. And I bet you have a case in your kitchen."

Jimmy's green masked bobbed up and down in agreement.

"All I'm saying," said Tommy, "is it hardly seems worth it."

Cassie held up a thin bar of lavender foil. "I scored a purple taffy. That's not nothing. My mom never lets me eat them."

"For good reason," said Tommy. "That's a turbo energy bar. It will mess you up."

"No, it won't," said Cassie, and defiantly poked the thin bar beneath her mask and tore off the top of the wrapper.

"Don't say I didn't warn ya," said Tommy.

"So if you don't like what we have, what else are we supposed to do?" asked Jimmy. "That's all there is on the station."

"Dat's not all dere is," said Cassie, chewing a chunk of taffy. "Julie said she heard dat Scram's were going to pass out foil-packed, chocolate covered brownies."

"There's brownies at the game shop?" asked Tommy.

"No, at the festival. She said Scram's flew in a whole pallet for Halloween to bring kids in."

"Then what are we waiting for? Let's go to the festival."

The Earth shone down brightly through the latticed skylight windows onto the mag-tiled ringed thoroughfare and the row shops lining either side, each storefront draped in synthetic webs and dangling rubber spiders and bats. Cauldrons and hollowed out jack-o-lantern bowls of treats were placed at most entrances, with the exception of the tailor and Scram's—the tailor was closed for the day, and Scram's had a sign in front that read *See you at the Arena*. Tommy led the way as the three crisscrossed to the left and right to snatch handfuls of the pudding paste that already filled their bags.

By the time the tri-colored robot team reached the causeway, a crowd had gathered and movement had as slowed the children from Lunar IV were joined by those from Lunar V coming the other way. When they turned the corner, they could see that the corridor to the hub was already overrun with costume clad children, full pillowcases in tow.

"Wow," said Jimmy. "Looks like everyone is heading to the festival. Do you think Scram's will have anything left?"

"Julie said they had tons," said Cassie.

"Yeah," said Tommy. "I wouldn't worry about it."

Above the crowd, the huge yellow and pink Lunar Arena sign slowly spun on its carousel, the colors washed out by the light of the Earth.

"I think the Earth is full," said Jimmy.

"So what?" said Tommy.

"It's just really rare. That's all."

"No it's not. I've seen the Earth a bazillion times."

"Not a full one," said Jimmy. "Not a hundred percent full disk."

"Hundred percent?" said Tommy. "A full Earth is a full earth."

"You'd know if you saw one. Especially on Halloween. My grandmother told me that's when it's most special."

"You're crazy," said Tommy. "Tell em', Cassie."

"I don't know," she said. She hadn't been paying much attention. "I'm feeling funny."

"It's because of that purple taffy," said Tommy.

Cassie pushed her glove against the bottom of her chest plate. She couldn't decide which was worse, the ache in her tummy or that Tommy was right.

"Take a deep breath," said Jimmy. "That'll help."

"Okay," she said, and drew a deep breath through her nose then let it out slowly. It helped, so she did it again. Her tummy instantly stopped quivering, but the deep breaths beneath the mask made her light headed, dreamy. She looked to either side, the momentum of the crowd moved them forward. She was floating within a river of masked children. Above her, the turning Lunar Arena sign passed overhead, replaced by the red ceiling of the entranceway, which then opened to the games arena. Above, centered in the grand dome, shining so bright it lit the stadium white, was the full earth. The lunar station's costumed army dissipated into the vastness of the arena, gathering at the many festival stands placed across the floor. Some were games, others exhibit, all had crowds, but the two longest queues were for the two Scram's stands, one for the brownies, the other for a large black cube.

"What's that?" Jimmy asked pointing at the cube. "And why is everyone walking out so wobbly?"

"It's Scram's new VR ride—*New York City*," said a passing ghost costumed child. "It's gravity ride," said the boy in the hero costume next to him. "You travel down to Earth and through the canyons of Manhattan," added the ghost.

"That sounds cool," said Tommy.

"Yeah, it's cool," said the ghost. "It will shred your stomach, but it's cool."

"The whole thing's in one G," said his friend. "They should call it the canyons of the damned."

"How do we get tickets?" asked Tommy.

The ghost pointed over to the other Scram's stand. "You get them over there. There's a bit of a wait, but it's worth it." He held up a foil square larger than his hand. "They have brownies," he said.

"Thanks," said Tommy, then to his robot cohorts, "Did you see that?"

"No kidding," said Jimmy. "It was huge."

"I told you," said Cassie. Her voice sounded week.

"Are you okay?" asked Jimmy.

"I'm fine," she said. "Let's get in line."

But she wasn't fine. Her tummy was aching again, and her skin was tingling. For a brief second, she was overwhelmed with lightness. The floor of the arena lifted and tilted. She thought she would faint, then, as suddenly as it started, it stopped; the room leveled and a wave of relief washed over her. Cassie shook her head and gazed upward. They were at the middle of the arena, the heart of the clear dome centered on the great disc.

"Are you sure you're okay?" Jimmy asked again.

"Yeah," said Tommy. "You're acting weird. If you don't want to ride the VR, that's okay. But you have to get your brownie."

"Are you kidding?" said Cassie. "I bet I strut out of there standing taller than you. I bet—"

A sharp pain stabbed her gut and she doubled over.

The room spun so hard that she dropped onto her hands and knees, and her helmet fell from her head. A million needles stabbed her from every direction.

She let out a muffled, pained, "Ahhh."

Then, as quickly as the last bout, she was okay—winded, but okay.

Cassie rolled onto her back. Tommy, Jimmy, and other kids from the line had circled around her and were whispering, "Oh wow," and, "Can you believe it," and, "Is this part of the show?"

"I'm so not eating one of those again," Cassie said as she propped herself up on her elbows. Nobody stepped away.

"Hey guys," said Cassie. "I'm okay. Can you give me some space?"

"You're not okay," said Jimmy.

"Whadda you talking about? The taffy made me dizzy. But I'm okay now. You're freaking me out."

Tommy lifted his mask. "You're not going to like this," he said.

"What?"

He rubbed the fur on his cheek in a manner suggesting she do the same.

She did. But her cheek was smooth—there was no fur.

As other children peeked over the shoulders of those who gathered first, there were more soft whispers of, "It can't be," and, "I don't believe it." The wolflings, one by one, raised their masks to get a better look, until all she could see was the bright Earth above and a halo of furry faces.

137

"This can't be," said Cassie. She tore away her gloves, then piece by piece, her armor, to find beneath only pink flesh.

By the light of the full Earth, Cassie had turned human.

ABOUT THE AUTHORS

Hunter C. Eden is a Denver-based essayist and dark fantasy writer whose work has appeared in *Weird Tales, City Slab*, and *Ravenous Monster Horror Webzine*.

Philip Harris was born in England but now lives in Canada where he works for a large video game developer. Not content with creating imaginary worlds for a living, he spends his spare time indulging his love of writing. His published books include **The Girl in the City Trilogy** and an homage to the old pulp science fiction serials - **Glitch Mitchell** and the **Unseen Planet**.
His short fiction has appeared in numerous anthologies and magazines including **The Jurassic Chronicles, Bones, Uncommon Minds, The Anthology of European SF**, and **Peeping Tom**. He has also worked as security for Darth Vader.

Jeff Bowles is a science fiction and horror writer from the mountains of Colorado. The best of his outrageous and imaginative short stories are collected in **Godling and Other Paint Stories, Fear and Loathing in Las Cruces**, and **Brave New Multiverse**. He has published work in magazines and anthologies like **PodCastle, Black Static, The Threepenny Review**, and **Dark Moon Digest**. Jeff earned his Master of Fine Arts degree in creative writing at Western State Colorado University. He currently lives in the high-altitude Pikes Peak region, where he dreams strange dreams and spends far too much time under the stars.

Michael Anthony Lee was has appeared in the 2017 anthology *Dreams of the Past* published by *Fantasia Divinity magazine*, and will be in their upcoming 2018 anthology *I will fight for You*.

Ernie Howard was born on January 29,1977 during a Minnesota blizzard. His two story telling parents almost didn't make it to the hospital in their beat up blue Cadillac. Ernie is the writer of *Write Something!*, a book about the illusion of Writers Block. *A World Without*, a Science Fiction book about the love between a husband and wife, and the darkness that can come into a marriage. *Walter*, A Science Fiction book about a boy who is an outcast who makes a friend with a man that speaks to him through his television. Ernie lives with his wife and 3 boys in Henderson, NV, where he dreams up new stories, and tries to live everyday to the fullest.

Desmond Warzel is the author of a few dozen short stories in the science fiction, fantasy, and horror genres. These have appeared in slick webzines such as *Abyss & Apex* and *Kaleidotrope*, on newfangled podcasts like *Escape Pod* and *The Drabblecast*, and on genuine dead tree in venerable magazines like *Fantasy & Science Fiction* and quality anthologies like *Spring into SciFi*. He lives in northwestern Pennsylvania where, when not writing, he follows the triumphs and tribulations of the Cleveland Indians (a pastime now slightly less futile than it used to be). When inevitably informed that the Indians are succeeding because they're in a weak division, he can only say, "It's about time."

David Alan Jones is a veteran of the US Air Force where he served as an Arabic linguist. He is also a martial artist, a husband, and a father of three. David writes novels that draw upon his experiences in intel and martial arts combined with his love of all things literary. An eclectic reader, David counts Anne Tyler, Stephen King, Lois McMaster Bujold, Robert J. Sawyer, J.K. Rowling and many others among his favorite, and most influential, authors.

Lorna Wood was raised in Oberlin, OH by a composer and an art historian. She received degrees in violin performance and English from Oberlin College and a Ph.D. in English from Yale University. After graduate school, she was an instructor for six years at Auburn University. In addition to *FAMILY VALUES*, Lorna's writing has appeared or is forthcoming in *CANYONS OF THE DAMNED, POETRY SOUTH, FIVE:2:ONE, SPECTACLE, WIKI LIT, FORMERCACTUS, POETRY WTF?! RUM PUNCH, JERRY JAZZ MUSICIAN, UNSTITCHED STATES, MYSTERICAL-E, SHUFPOETRY, BETWEEN WORLDS ZINE, WILD VIOLET, CACTI FUR, BIRDS PILED LOOSELY, EVERY WRITER, BLUE MONDAY REVIEW, and the anthologies LEAVES OF LOQUAT IV (Loquat Literary Festival), LUMINOUS ECHOES (INTO THE VOID MAGAZINE),* and *DARK MAGIC (Owl Hollow Press)*, among others. In 2018 she won second prize in the Loquat Literary Festival poetry contest; in 2017 she was a finalist in the *JERRY JAZZ MUSICIAN* contest; and in 2016 she was shortlisted for *INTO THE VOID's* poetry competition and a finalist in the Neoverse Short Story Competition and the Valus' Sigil contest at *SHARKPACK POETRY REVIEW.* Her poetry has been favorably reviewed on *NEW PAGES.* Lorna has published scholarly essays on the American Renaissance and children's literature, and she is currently Associate Editor of *GEMINI MAGAZINE.*

Robert Jeschonek According to Mike Resnick, Robert Jeschonek "is a towering talent." Robert is an award-winning writer whose fiction, comics, essays, articles, and podcasts have been published around the world. His young adult fantasy novel, *My Favorite Band does not Exist*, won the Forward National Literature Award and was named one of BOOKLIST's Top Ten First Novels for Youth. His cross-genre science fiction thriller, *Day 9*, is an International Book Award winner. He also won the 2013 Scribe Award for Best Original Novel from the International Association of Media Tie-in Writers for his alternate history, *Tannhäuser: Rising Sun, Falling Shadows*. Simon & Schuster, DAW/Penguin Books, and DC Comics have published his work. He won the grand prize in Pocket Books' nationwide Strange New Worlds contest and was nominated for the British Fantasy Award.

Will Swardstrom is a speculative fiction author. His latest novel is *Blink*, the first adventure in *The Utility Company* series, co-written with his brother Paul. He also has two full length novels, *Dead Sleep* and *Dead Sight*, and is at work on the finale in the trilogy. He also has three stories in The Future Chronicles anthology series (*Uncle Allen* in *The Alien Chronicles*, *Z Ball* in *The Z Chronicles*, and *The Control* in *The Immortality Chronicles*). Each of those anthologies has charted in the Top 5 on the SF Anthology list and The Alien Chronicles reached as high as #6 on the Overall Top 100 List. The Control from The Immortality Chronicles has been nominated for Best American Science Fiction. He also has a few stories set in Hugh Howey's WOOL Universe among his various other short stories and novellas. He lives in Southern Illinois with his wife and two kids.

Jessica West (a.k.a. West1Jess) is currently pursuing a state of self-induced psychosis, also known as writing. In the past, she has worked for Wal-Mart, a lawyer, and a bank. Now if she could just get a couple years experience with the IRS and the NSA, world domination is in the bag.

Jess lives in Acadiana with three daughters still young enough to think she's cool and a husband who knows better but likes her anyway.

For more information, visit west1jess.com.

Daniel Arthur Smith is a USA Today bestselling author. His titles include ***Spectral Shift, Hugh Howey Lives, The Cathari Treasure, The Somali Deception***, and a few other novels and short stories. He also curates the phenomenal short fiction series ***Tales from the Canyons of the Damned*** and ***Frontiers of Speculative Fiction***.

He was raised in Michigan and graduated from Western Michigan University where he studied philosophy, with focus on cognitive science, meta-physics, and comparative religion. He began his career as a bartender, barista, poetry house proprietor, teacher, and then became a technologist and futurist for the Fortune 100 across the Americas and Europe.

Daniel has traveled to over 300 cities in 22 countries, residing in Los Angeles, Kalamazoo, Prague, Crete, and now writes in Manhattan where he lives with his wife and young sons.

For more information, visit danielarthursmith.com